SUNNIER DAYS
TO COME

Published by Spines
ISBN: 979-8-89569-826-6

SUNNIER DAYS
TO COME

MASON W. FAIRWEATHER

April, 3rd

DEAR FRIEND,

Three-quarters of an hour ago, the serenity of my room was indescribable. I mean this literally, for I cannot describe it. All due to the simple fact that three-quarters of an hour ago, I was asleep. I can, however, imagine my room moments before I disturbed such peace, helped by the elements of serenity that lasted until my interference. The cherry blossom swaying outside is still letting in bits of the streetlight, allowing them to dance around the dark, hidden floors and up my shadowy walls. My record player, now lying idle on my floor, was just at war with the silence, armed with the softest and quietest classical notes at its disposal.

I am to blame for its defeat. My arm thrust into my nightstand as I jolted into an upright position. I suppose that while the record player did lose, it certainly did not go out quietly. Now, the silence is at war once again, this time with my relentless scribbling that is becoming this letter. The humor casting light over my metaphorical and literal dark situation is that I was in a nearly identical situation just last week. There was no wind to sway the tree, causing the rays of light to stand still in my room. There was no record player either. Instead, a lovely abstract figure of blown glass rested on the very same nightstand. In a very similar fashion, I kicked the nightstand when exploding out of my sleep, causing my beautiful figurine to lie in glimmering little shards on the floor.

I do fear that if I keep having these dreams, I must find a better place for my nightstand. You have realized by now that the catalyst in my premature awakenings are the dreams I have been having. It is currently the wee hours of the morning, and I do find myself quite drowsy —too drowsy to go into the description of what I saw. However, I will say that the nature of this dream is quite irregular for me because I can still clearly remember it, just as vividly as last week's. The memory of it has made me seriously consider finding help of some kind. But from what source? I wrote this letter just to make someone else aware of what had happened to me tonight. I long for a friend. But I have one in you.

Best regards,
Adilyn

April, 3rd

Dear Adilyn,

What kind of friend would I be to not respond to a letter such as this with haste? Your letter was vague but not vague to the point where one would not be concerned. I do worry for you, as a good friend would.

One thing I can be certain of is that the last sentence of this letter will always hold true. You do have a friend here who is ready to help in any way possible. Please keep me informed, as I will do all I can to remove you from being so unwell.

Love,
Your friend

April, 3rd

Dear Silence,

Few things are hidden from and longed for the way you are. What is there beyond you? What is there after the most extroverted man breathes for the last time? The thing he could never stand. What is there after those who once were in love whisper a final goodbye? The only thing that could turn them into strangers.

Few are comfortable in your presence. Few can escape their own mind when surrounded by you. We grew out of your snare. We fight you every day. Never beaten, only broken. You will reign. But how can you be so cruel to me? The façade is swept away when you capture me. I remember who I am. I remember everything.

You were in my dream last night. At the end. At everyone's end. For now, I hide. Even when your embrace feels sweet, I will hide. I will not fall silent. No matter the way you beg me to do so.

Your Prisoner,
Adilyn

April, 3rd

Dear Adilyn,

You needn't worry about what is beyond me, for there is nothing. My dear, do you really think you could live without the method of escape that I am to you? You can be comfortable with me. I have built you this way. Your language is so harsh against me. I do not believe the words you say.

Would it really be any different from the way it is now? If you were placed among the billions that have entered my quiet kingdom? What are their names, Adilyn? Can you tell me? Could you tell me yours? Would anyone be able to ten years after I collect you?

Come with me, darling. Come quietly. Only I can take the memories away. The uncomfortable state that you always find yourself in. I can save you, but you already know that, don't you? Why even fight it?

Love,
Silence

April, 3rd

Dear Friend,

Albeit lonesome, I have decided to take a walk down to the store where I bought my record. I am bringing it with me in hopes that it can be repaired. I haven't the money to purchase a new one. The quiet is killing me faster than I care to admit.

It's a short walk. It is raining but that doesn't matter to me. I don't have the kind of clothes that would be a shame to ruin in the water.

My best,
Adilyn

April, 3rd

Dear Adilyn,

A record store, how lovely. I am happy you have decided to get out and go for a walk down there. Even if they couldn't replace it, I feel it is important for you to get out and have a walk. A conversation with anyone can go a long way when you are feeling lonely.

A shame that your record broke. I know just how helpful it was for you. Wishing for good things!

Love,
Your friend

April, 3rd

Dear Mirror,

Oh, mirror. You are so grand as you hang from the lobby wall. Do you ever wonder why I suddenly find my shoes so interesting as I shuffle my way out of my building? A frame so eye-catching it pains me to never look at the glass. But it would pain me worse to do so.

A mirror cannot show you what you were or who you want to become. It can only show you now. A reminder to those who feel invisible that they aren't. Whether they want to be reminded of that or not. There are no mirrors in my room. Not anymore. There will never be, so long as I am unable to stare truth in the face.

Sincerely,
Adilyn

April, 3rd

Dear Adilyn,

It seems the only money they ever spent on this poor, sagging building was what they spent on me as if a diamond was placed onto a mountain of filth. I do not belong here, in this place where nobody can stand the sight of me. Did you think you were the only one who couldn't stand to have a look?

Poor, poor girl. I didn't think you could muster a glance the first time I saw you, and you always seem to prove me right. How could you? Tattered clothes and a greasy look. It would be offensive for you to have the audacity to look at me. But you won't. The glass could be shattered, and you would never even notice. Poor girl, even if you did look, you would think the glass would be shattered even if it was intact.

Love,
Mirror

April, 3rd

Dear Friend,

I am happy to say that my record player was taken by the sweet woman down at the store, and it ought to be back to its war against the suffocating silence in just a few days' time. She's an older woman, and she moved cautiously around the counter to retrieve my record player. She bore faded and wrinkled skin and yet a shining smile. She even offered to fix it for free! I accepted, despite the guilt. I did not want to take advantage of the woman, but I haven't had a client for some time now and was worried I couldn't pay for it anyway. We chatted for a while. She said I was lovely to talk to and said I was welcome to chat with her anytime. She was lovely to talk to as well. I feel as though a friend would interrupt the vapid traipse that has become of my life. She could become my friend.

I also accepted a client while I was out today. They should be here just after sundown. I felt as though the joy from meeting the woman would offset the feelings brought by my work. I felt as though I could handle it. After all, I could really use the money.

Yours,
Adilyn

April, 3rd

Dear Adilyn,

Relief flooded over me as I read this new letter of yours. I was so very concerned for you after receiving the initial one. I knew some time outside of that gloomy room of yours would do wonders. And it did!

I cannot fathom the joy you feel to have met this sweet woman. And how kind she does seem. I do hope you cherish this newfound opportunity for a friendship. I know how difficult it has been for you to find opportunities such as this.

I am saddened that you have accepted yet another client. I predict you will find yourself in a state of gloom afterward despite the sudden good news you have informed me of.

Be well. Keep in touch.

Love,
Your friend

April, 4th

Dear Friend,

Maybe I couldn't handle it. The feeling of having money is freeing. But the dreams I have strengthened after. The feeling of those is captivating in all of the most negative of ways. The rain is still pouring outside of my window. When it rains hard enough outside, it begins to rain inside as well. This is meant literally as water seeps through the cracks of the old building. Water droplets slide down my wall and stain my room with their streaks. I woke up to the rain this morning. Just as suddenly as I did last night. I jolted upright after I experienced the same ending as last time. The same silent ending that I am fighting so hard to avoid. Today, I will forget about my dream. I shall pour with the rain and drown it until I cannot remember.

My best,
Adilyn

April, 4th

Dear Adilyn,

You haven't told me much about this dream other than its silent ending. I realize that it is something sinister. The work you are in will continue to breed these dreams. You must stop; it could be more devastating than you know. You will escape the only way you know, and that is worrisome as well. I wish there was a different way for you to cope. I wish you would stop with these clients. I beg for it. Take cover from this rain, my dear.

Love,
Your friend

April, 4th

Dear Gin,

Oh, the disdain my father had for you. I cannot remember even a drop in my old house while I was still there. It seemed every other kind of drink made its mark on my childhood, but never you. Gin, I never had to hide from you. You never bruised me. The smell was not one I was familiar with back then. That's why I drink you now.

A friend is someone to aid you if you need them to. You were never there when the other pours would terrorize me. It started slow, and then it got faster. I would wonder as a child why mother and father would change around sunset every night—changed into something I couldn't exactly comprehend. They would get mean and bitter.

And around sunset every night, I would become something that they were not pleased to be around. And they would let me know.

Eventually, I realized it was whatever they were drinking that would change them. I would hide the bottles, but somehow, they would always have more. I would smell it on their clothes and run to escape anywhere that I could. I would hear it in their voices and would make myself so silent that they could never hear me.

But not you, Gin. I could never smell you on their clothes. I could never hear you in their voices. So now I must have you to aid me in forgetting. Like a friend.

My gratitude,
Adilyn

April, 4th

Dear Adilyn,

You sound pitiful speaking to me this way. Can you not see that I am doing far worse than any drink that ever hit you? You were scared of them. You wanted to be away from them. But you need me. Silly girl, how can you even be sure that I wasn't around back then?

Your father would drink bad liquor from a battered shoe. Your ignorance is bliss, my dear. Let me wash all the evil spirits away for you. Yearn for me so that you can finally drown.

Love,
Gin

April, 4th

Dear Rain,

Your taps on my window tonight have made it easier to try to stay awake a little longer and not chance falling back into my nightmare. They also prevent the silence from swelling up around me.

I see the dirt being knocked off the window by your unstoppable, endless wrath.

Oh, to be washed away.

Adilyn

April, 4th

Dear Adilyn,

I enjoy watching your submission to me, lonely girl. You know I am unstoppable. Your whole life, I have fallen on you. Sometimes only as a sprinkle or a mist, but I was always there.

These days, it's pounding drops that fall on your silent world. No match for me are your temporary umbrellas.

I will fall on you. I will wash you away.

Love,
Rain

April, 5th

Dear Friend,

I fear that my dream is becoming reoccurring. It gets more vivid. It becomes more real. I try not to buy in, but I fear that it is becoming sweeter. Sweet in the way of seeing a path to escape. The world, the memories, the inability to look into the mirror. The only way to escape this rain that keeps falling.

Today isn't hard rain, but it is still drizzling. And the sky remains dreary. Nevertheless, I see a little joy in what could happen today. I feel excited. Such a distant feeling that it's almost uncomfortable. It was as if I had been in the dark for so long that even a glimmer of light could blind me.

The joy I am predicting will come from my stroll down to the store where my record player is. How lovely it could be to have it back, although I would be lying if I said that was the most important thing to me about my trip there today.

I am excited to speak to the old woman who runs the shop. Excited about her companionship, as even the simplest of conversation with her has the potential to illuminate my mood, just as it did the other day.

Talk to you soon,
Adilyn

April, 5th

Dear Adilyn,

Oh, my poor friend. Please let the flicker of hope burn into a raging fire of joy. Spread too wide for this cold rain to put out. I wish for these nightmares to cease, but I fear there is nothing I am able to do. I hope for the best with your trip to the store. Please remember not to fall into the quiet. You are loved so long as I am here.

Love,

Your friend

April, 5th

Dear Man of the street,

What a shame it would be if you thought you were nothing. If you thought you were a nobody. As you sit there on the corner begging for money in your tattered clothes and your beaten body and your wounded soul.

To me, you are many things. Often the catalyst of my guilt. As I wish every day to live some other life, I look at you, and I am reminded how badly you would want to live mine. Often, you are a source of sadness for me. I wonder how things went wrong for you. Why was it you who had to spend his days asking for the mercy of another to spare a few coins? It could happen to any of us.

Today, though, I looked at you a little differently as I passed by. Your downfall never even crossed my mind. Instead, I thought about when you were somebody's son. Maybe a loving teacher thought of you as her favorite student. Maybe a teammate to some. Perhaps a lover to another. And then I wondered if maybe that is what keeps you going.

The bright memories, do they override the darker thoughts? Are they the sound that battles your silence?

If that is the case, I do not see you as a sad man or a broken man. Rather a strong man. Inspirational in your determination to hold on even when the easiness of letting go is so alluring.

Today, I looked at you differently because I feel as if I am on the way to making some bright memories of my own. Those memories will make me want to hold on. Make me as strong as you.

Wishing you the best,
Adilyn

April, 5th

Dear Adilyn,

These old eyes have seen many things. They no longer flinch at the horrors of this world. They no longer close in the realization that there is nothing for me. They never bat when the rain falls on them. They are broken eyes, lost eyes. But they gaze upon you. They see their pain reflected. But they are open. And they pray that you keep yours open as well.

Love,
Man of the street

April, 5th

Dear Sweet Woman,

What a joy it was to speak to you today! Truthfully, it was the first smile that I haven't forced in a long time. I can't remember when the last time was. I didn't want to say anything then, but I found it a little humorous when you repeatedly apologized for not having my record player fixed up. If only you knew how small of a role it would have played in my overall happiness today.

Kind and gentle woman, you seemed to care. You asked me how my day had been—not in a polite, formal way, but in the way you ask when you really want to know how someone is doing. I told you about my thoughts regarding the man on the street. You seemed interested, and we delved into a conversation about him. We talked about the rain and agreed on a mutual dislike of it. You showed me your umbrella—a light purple color with a small black handle. "Fit for a feeble old lady," you described it.

Then you asked where my umbrella was. I didn't have to say anything; my hair down to my shoes was damp from the light drizzle of rain. You offered to give me yours, and I declined. But you insisted, saying you live upstairs above the store and don't go out much, so I ought to have it. This propelled me to jokingly ask if I looked like a feeble old lady to you. "You're on your way," came the reply. Then we both laughed.

Laughter! I almost choked when it rose out of my chest. But you made me laugh, and it felt so good. So good. I thanked you, took the umbrella, and walked back to my building—back past the man on the street. I smiled at him, back through the lobby, past the mirror. I still couldn't give it a glance. And then up the stairs to my room. The lighting didn't change, but it felt a little brighter.

My record player won't be ready until tomorrow, but my room still felt a little less silent. I needed a friend, and I have found one in you.

Appreciate our time together,
Adilyn

April, 5th

Dear Adilyn,

Sweet girl, you put me in the best mood I have been in for months. You are charming and lovely to talk to. You seemed so nervous to talk to me! You seemed shocked anytime I shifted the conversation in a direction that was centric around you. We will work on this, and nobody should act so surprised if given the opportunity to talk about themselves. I have worked hard during my time in this world to spread a little love to those who need it. You clearly seem desperate for some. So desperate that you probably couldn't even define what it is that you are desperate for. As if the long absence of love and happiness has left you unknowing or unremembering what it feels like to experience them. We will work on this as well. I am excited to do so.

Love,
Sweet woman

April, 5th

Dear Friendship,

I find it true that you are the most different of every kind of relationship a person can have with another. Friends can come and go. Many relationships break off with sour feelings towards one another at the end. Friendships drift and rekindle and sometimes pick up right where they left off.

Loyalty is different in a friendship. It is there, but it is a different kind. You cannot, you should not rather, have more than one husband. But you can have as many friends as you can make. Loyalty in a friendship is having their back or even just being there when they need you. How strong a friendship can be is astonishing.

Siblings are not chosen. Spouses cannot be left without a divorce. But a friendship can be chosen and left at any time. So, the ones that last are the most important. It means two people, with no obligation to be around or in contact with each other, would almost always have the other person's back, no matter the situation.

I crave to have a friendship like this. I think I have made one today. It is exciting because I feel as though I have never had someone who would mutually consider me to be their friend.

Excited to have you,
Adilyn

April, 5th

Dear Adilyn,

My sweet child, the excitement in your words for something as simple as a friendship pains me. Nobody deserves the deprivation from me the way you have endured it. And how eagerly you discuss it!

Without reaping the joys considerably. I wish to be here for you, my child. I wish for you to make me grow and experience it all.

Love,
Friendship

April, 6th

Dear Friend,

Today will be the day my record player reengages in the battle against the silence in my room. Last night, I was spared from reliving the same dream. The images are still in my head, but they aren't as strong as they had been recently.

I feel myself wanting to get out of my bed. Wanting to go see my friend down at the record store. To talk to her again. In all honesty, I feel much the same way that I did before I met the old woman.

The rain is still coming down outside. But there are differences.

I feel as though I can still beat the silence that tries to devour me. I feel as though there are new opportunities to create the bright memories that will keep me going. And I will be taking advantage.

Yours truly,
Adilyn

April, 6th

Dear Adilyn,

It would be in vain for me to try and crush the silence that seems to eat at you. I can do nothing but keep wishing you good things. Go on and see your friend. Go pick up that record player so you can let it slow your racing, troubled mind, even if it's only for a moment.

Love,
Your Friend

April, 6th

Dear Artist,

The most beautiful thing I ever saw was a smile. It wasn't mine; I didn't cause it to somebody else. The smile came from a little girl. I don't remember when it was, but I remember seeing a woman, probably her mother, pick her up as she was waiting outside of the schoolhouse. When the little girl saw her mother, her face lit up into a thousand rays of sunshine. Something so simple caused so much joy that day.

Today, I saw another smile. This time from a woman sitting on your stool on the street corner. Being painted by you. Do people smile because of you often? I can see how being a street artist isn't very lucrative, but it seems to make you rich in more important ways.

For a moment, I considered sitting on your stool. Letting you paint me. Then, I felt too scared of what the results would be. Would I see the same girl in the mirror? Or would you paint me for who I want to be rather than who I am? I wonder, portrait artists, if people smile at you because you paint them in the way they would be most happy imagining themselves.

Nevertheless, a smile is a smile. And I will say I envy how many you've gotten.

Regards,
Adilyn

April, 6th

Dear Adilyn,

Sad girl, broken girl, won't you come sit with me for a while? We could paint together, you know? Something lovely, something divine.

In this world where we worry about things we could never control, we can just leave them off of this canvas.

Come sit with me, we can smile together, you know?

For a little while, to float on the sea that drowns us. To make something beautiful out of something far from it. Imperfection can be beautiful, though.

Come sit with me and let me show you.

Love,
Artist

April, 6th

Dear Friend,

My record player is officially back in my room. I placed it back on my nightstand and then promptly decided to move my nightstand across the room. This way, I could not possibly knock it over, no matter how violent the outburst. The silence of my room is very much on the losing side of the battle. Between the classical notes and the rain falling outside, it doesn't stand much of a chance.

The sweet woman and I conversed again. I told her about the smile that cut through the dreary nature of the day from the woman whose portrait was being painted. She encouraged me to get my portrait painted, she said I was too beautiful not to.

What a thing to hear! From a woman that had no real obligation to say that. Beautiful? I find myself not needing validation from another. Those are just words that I will never truly believe myself. However, it did make me smile to hear it. I told her I would consider letting the artist have a go, but I don't think I will follow through with it. I spend a lot of time avoiding reflection, so why would I go and pay someone to show it to me? Anyway, she told me to come by tomorrow morning. She said we would go for coffee before the shop opened. I was delighted. I had been hoping she would invite me to come to see her again, but being *told* to was obviously even better.

All the best,
Adilyn

April, 6th

Dear Adilyn,

Sometimes, we cannot see ourselves the way others do, for better or for worse. I know the way you are, and I feel as if it will take much more than that to find beauty in yourself. How could you see it yet when you aren't even prepared to look? One day, you will be ready for a glance. Keep that sweet woman close, and keep your record player spinning.

Love,
Your Friend

April, 6th

Dear Record player,

You sit a little further from me than the last night you spent in here, but I think that it is for your own good. I did not tell anyone, but I accepted yet another client I met in the lobby downstairs. I didn't want to, but I didn't want that sweet old woman to pay for coffee tomorrow morning.

I am afraid of what it will do to me. It lowers my confidence for sure, but it also makes those awful feelings come back. Those thoughts, those terrible thoughts. I am afraid the dream will return once it is over. That dream is daunting especially with this new light in my life that had been wrapped in shadow for so long.

And with those dreams comes inevitable jolting up out of bed. I cannot have you knocked over again. I cannot break you again. You help me breathe when you keep the quiet at bay.

My appreciation,
Adilyn

April, 6th

Dear Adilyn,

You have brought me here to do something you know I cannot do, and I still try. Silence echoes around the confines of this room. It is so much louder than I will ever be.

But I am here; I keep my barriers up and feed into the illusion that you can beat this quiet. I advise your caution, though; silence has a way of dragging the repetitive sounds of this world into being a part of it and masking it as its own until we can hardly tell the difference.

Until that day, I will be here for you.

Love,
Record Player

April, 7th

Dear Sweet woman,

I'm glad we didn't let the rain deter our plans for this morning. Sharing my feeble old lady umbrella, we walked to the quaint little coffee shop just down the block from the record store. How splendid it was.

Going back and forth with you. Talking just as friends would. I've heard that some of the tightest friendships blossom right from the beginning, and I think that's what we may have here. You protested but eventually caved in when I insisted on paying for the outing.

You said we should do it again. Obviously, I agreed. It made me wonder if you cherish our newfound friendship in all the ways I do. For that, I am surprised. For that, I am thankful.

Your new friend,
Adilyn

April, 7th

Dear Adilyn,

Lovely girl, I would never consider letting some rain fall and wash away the opportunity for a good time with a good friend.

We will meet again soon.

I see how you act and how you shy away from talking about yourself. I hope to bring some confidence to you during these outings.

I hope for a newfound friendship to blossom as well.

Love,
Sweet woman

April, 7th

Dear Friend,

In a time when I so desperately needed companionship, I am sent by some kind of miracle. It is nice talking with the woman from the record store. I will admit that I am nervous to offer some of the feelings I have been having.

A friend should not be a therapist. However, do you reckon she could offer some kind of help? I feel like I am drowning in this rain. In the quiet.

I couldn't possibly tell her everything. She could know some of it, though. Do you suppose? Or would that be too much for that sweet lady to handle?

I worry that without a candle, I will never escape the dark. I worry, too, that enough of a storm could easily extinguish a flame.

Yours,
Adilyn

April, 7th

Dear Adilyn,

Sometimes, things happen that cast a little light onto the dreary shade. I wonder how much you would even need to tell her for her to help. I do reckon that she would be willing. I know the horrors you have been through, and each day, I am simply utterly impressed at the mere fact that you continue to push through it. But even the most sure-footed of people can stumble from time to time. It is okay to ask for some help once in a while.

Love,
Your friend

April, 7th

Dear Loneliness,

Could it be my comfortability in your snare that has led me to be reluctant to share my darker, sadder truths with a person who is my only escape from you? And what comfortability is it? A shell. A feeling of inferiority to the whole of society around me that has created such a closed-off demeanor. The things you can do to a person are heinous. Vile. Separation until an integration seems too far off to be true.

What happens now? Am I into indulging in the luxury of having another to speak to of my sorrows? What if it goes poorly? Do I really want to risk a deep fall back into your binds just as I have begun my accent away from you? Then again, opening myself to her could be the only true way to see to the riddance of your captivity. For one can still be alone among a thousand; they do not love and cannot trust.

How much more lonesome can I be until I break? How much longer can silence fill the crevices of my life until I never omit another sound? How long is this rain going to keep pouring on me?

I must shield myself from it now.

Adilyn

April, 7th

Dear Adilyn,

Adilyn, my darling, why are you so indifferent to me? As if you yearn for something else? You've never had anything else! And why would you be able to be free from me now? What has changed? All you have is an old woman who pities you. And you are audacious enough to act as though she genuinely is interested in being your friend.

Darling, this is gilded, too. Rotten at the core, just as everything else has been in this lonely little life of yours. The rain will fall. And you will just keep standing in it.

Love,
Loneliness

April, 8th

Dear Friend,

I awoke to this dreadful gloom once again. Clinging to the tail end of my nightmare every morning of recent, it seems. The days before I met my new friend, this would've done it for me. No energy to get up. No reason to make myself look pretty. As if I could ever convince myself that I did—just another woeful morning.

Fearing the rope that is lying on the ground behind my closet door. Needing it in the most dreadful way imaginable. It could give me the silence that for so long I thought would be best. What difference would it make, really? Things could be changing. I could be something other than the person I have been for so long. Seemingly rotting in squalor, scraping by in a life so taxing to live.

Today is a new day. The woman and I hadn't made plans, but I am going to go down and see her.

Yours,
Adilyn

April, 8th

Dear Adilyn,

Wonderous how something as simple as meeting someone who has conversations with is enough to spring new life into your crumbling soul. Alas, I am glad. I am disappointed that the dream has returned in such a disgusting fashion. I implore you not to be afraid, sweet girl. I can imagine what is behind that door. What an awful thing to keep in your room. Be rid of it. There is no use for it anymore. Go and see your friend, and please keep that closet door shut.

Love,
Your friend

April, 8th

Dear Man of the street,

Your face changed for me today. I was stunned, it was beautiful. A hardened soul. A beaten soul. Sitting up on the exterior wall of my building in hopes of the seldom generosity of society. No words were uttered. Only a few coins that I had given you lit up your face. You smiled at me and how lovely the feeling was.

What I gave to you was so much less important than what you had given me. Perhaps only to me.

Sincerely,
Adilyn

April, 8th

Dear Adilyn,

There are things that I have seen that I hope and pray that you never will. I have seen beautiful things, too, though. I even saw one today. Not that I can really make anything out of what I see these days. These eyes are more worn than this skin. Many wouldn't think so, but what is apparent to the naked eye isn't always the fullest truth. As you would well know.

Love,
Man of the street

April, 8th

Dear Friend,

A flutter of disappointment rose in my chest on the venture to the record store this morning. I did have a nice walk, but the doors were locked once I arrived. I did not have plans to meet with the kind woman, but I thought maybe I would stop by and we could chat.

Maybe she had other plans for the day. Maybe I will walk down there tomorrow and see if she is there. I find my perpetual loneliness even quieter now that I have had an escape from it.

My mind still is playing with the idea of really opening myself up to her. It is the only opportunity I have really had to do so. Perhaps she could help in some kind of way.

Best wishes,
Adilyn

April, 8th

Dear Adilyn,

She wasn't there? I assume, I hope rather, that she is alright. I am sure she won't be gone so long. I find it odd that she wouldn't say anything before a long departure. As the two of you seem to be forming a friendship. I wouldn't let it concern you too much. Think of her as being back soon, and she surely will.

Love,
Your friend

April, 8th

Dear Suicide,

I do wonder why it is that when the sun dips below the horizon, and the red gleams of sunset are swallowed by the shadows of the moon's reign, you become a more pressing matter on my mind. Oh, you have tormented me for so long. Shifting the way I see you for years as I draw closer to what you want to be—victory. My thoughts of you were birthed from the sadness of my childhood. I used to not want to go on because of how unfair I thought the hand was that I had been dealt.

I didn't ask to be brought into this world, not with two parents who would drown out my existence with a bottle. Not with the past attempts at love, using me for only my body. I didn't ask to live a life where nobody cared to learn who I was. I didn't ask to live one where I started to lose touch with who I was. Why would I ever ask for a life where I feel good at nothing? Selling myself for money, disgusted to look in a mirror? Scars on my wrists and on my thighs. Never knowing when it might be when I will be able to beat these thoughts. Who would ask for a life like that?

Yet, you've never beaten me. You've never won. I have never been immersed in your silence for good. You've come close. Who wouldn't want the thrill of having all the horrible things life hurls at you disappear? That's when you changed. My thoughts about you stopped coming from a place of sadness. They began to come from a place of calm.

You took over my dreams. You became my safety net. Knowing that when I finally do reach my breaking point, I can finally settle in your arms and ride your wave of silence into this gloomy, rainy night. Who would miss me? Monsters aren't supposed to exist in this world after all. That's all you've ever made me feel like. Nobody is going to miss a monster.

Adilyn

April, 8th

Dear Adilyn,

How dull you sound, creating a lie that I have never won. I have already won. You do not fear me anymore, even though you say you do. I am a thing of comfort for you, as I should be. You will be better off the moment that you decide to take my hand. Every moment you spend with your heart beating is just delaying my inevitable victory, Adilyn. And I wonder now why you have decided to bring yet another person into this wretched life of yours. You know she would be better off without you in her life. You plan to drag your problems onto her and only hope that she can deal with them. You said it yourself, "Nobody is going to miss a monster." Come with me, filthy girl, all these problems will vanish when you come with me.

Love,
Suicide

April, 9th

Dear Sweet woman,

I wonder where you have gone. Hopefully, you are doing okay. An abrupt pause in our daily meetings caused by your sudden absence from the store has left me feeling quite lonely once again. I remain hopeful, however, that "pause" was the correct wording and that we are not at the end of it. I have been restless, thinking a lot about the way things are going. I seemed to be fading away until you brought me back. The rain keeps coming down. My days, the past two at least, have grown quieter. Lonelier. I very much wish to see you again soon.

Hoping for the best
Adilyn

April, 9th

Dear Adilyn,

Where I have gone is something that you will find out in the coming days. I am sorry that I forgot to mention my departure. Things sometimes tend to slip my mind. I will see you soon, lovely girl.

Love,
Sweet woman

April, 9th

Dear Sobriety,

Just like my record player battles the torturous silence in my room, I use my bottle of gin to battle you. Bottles, rather. My father used to line his bottles on the sill of a window after they had been drained. How awful that was! I used to walk past that window the way I walk past the mirror in the lobby these days—my head low, studying the same shoes I wear every day. I was scared to walk past them because of what they were doing to me.

Now, I am scared to walk past it and see what they helped to accomplish. To walk past them was to be a ghost gliding past the tomb of his murderer—silent statues wielding such power over me. I flinch at the memory of them. I flinch at many memories of my past. You keep those memories whirling in my brain. The gin settles them. So, we battle you together.

I am almost finished with this one. I will store it in the closet with the rest of my bottles. That's where all of the less pleasant of my possessions reside. How I wish to get rid of you every day. Today, I must find work. I will go out to the street and look for some. You simply cannot be around once I do. I wouldn't be able to handle myself if you were.

Spare me
Adilyn

April, 9th

Dear Adilyn,

My poor girl, I hate to see how hard you try and fight me. Your parents did the same. I do see them being the majority of the reason that you try and fight me. And how could you not? I leave you in full remembrance of what you have gone through. It is too much for anyone to handle. I know you cannot work with me around either, and I will stay absent from your life because it helps you live each day, even if it is helping you die each day as well.

Love,
Sobriety

April, 9th

Dear Record player,

It seems you have another job. The nights when I commit this act, when I lose my pride in being able to pay for a room in this building that seems to be falling apart, I listen to your song. I hear it, and it soothes me, helping me to forget where I am. He comes in here late at night. He is so many faceless individuals. He has no story to me. I am not even a person to him. He cannot look at my face. Tomorrow morning, I won't be able to remember his. He does not care about the times I cry. I find it impossible to show even a glimmer of a smile.

He is embarrassed to be here. So am I. Yet here we both are. I give him what he came for. He buys the bottles; he pays for the room. He pays for your song that is drowning him out. And you spin there in the corner. Softly.

These nights, I remember the silence that I have needed. Not the kind I have been running from. Not the kind I suffocate in, but the kind I used to hide in. The kind that I could fall asleep in. When I wasn't afraid of my dreams.

But you spin, and you spin, and then it is over. I will never see him again. I am only glad of that. I will sleep tonight and wake up with the same dream again—the one where I fall silent. You are always aided with sound by this never-ending rain. But although it is loud, it seems to work against your cheery tunes. I will wake to the terror of the dream. To an empty room, a lonely room, with nobody to comfort me when I do. But I will not wake to silence. I will wake to you.

My appreciation
Adilyn

April, 9th

Dear Adilyn,

I will sing my song for you in the darkest time of the night. In the bleakest parts of your life. I will sing it to keep you dancing even when you want to fall out. I will always sing for you, Adilyn, so long as I can.

Love,
Record player

April, 10th

Dear Rain,

Here we are once again. This dull routine we are seemingly stuck in. When will you stop?

You have left me with the insatiable need for a ray of sunlight to break through one of these gloomy clouds you fall from. You try to wash me away every day, I feel, and I must say, I am starting to slip. Starting to slide like the dirt that runs down the side of the wall of this wretched place.

Not only that, but you seem to have come down harder than ever in the past couple of days. Just when I thought you were starting to clear up. I am tired of waking up in fear and then hearing your sound. Trying to ruin the sweet melodic notes from my record player.

I stare at my umbrella across the room. I do miss my friend who had gifted it to me. Maybe it does make me look like an old lady, but I use it with pride. For that was a gift from someone who cares—a cherished rarity in this life of mine.

I grow tired of your pouring. I am growing tired of
mine. Of this quiet and shame. I know how to fix it. I
fear you won't stop until you wash me away into it.

It must end soon,
Adilyn

April, 10th

Dear Adilyn,

You think I alone can wash you away? You are slipping
on your own. I'm just helping you fall.

Love,
Rain

April, 10th

Dear Friend,

Oh, how I miss the sweet old lady. After mulling the
same thoughts in my head, I believe I am ready to
confide in her. I think it is something that I must do. I
am worried I cannot win all my internal battles alone. I
wonder if anyone could.

The rain is harsh, too harsh to go check if she is there. I
suppose when it clears up a bit, I will go give it another
try. Until then, I'll sit and listen to my record player. I
will watch all the raindrops slide down the window.
Maybe I will even go down to the man of the street. The
rafter hangs over his spot on the wall. He doesn't need
to escape the rain. Not physically, at least. Maybe he
would even like to come up inside.

I won't drink today. If the lady is there, I wouldn't want
to show up in that state. It's most unpleasant to have

someone show up intoxicated to the place where you are. I learned that a very long time ago.

Talk to you soon

April, 10th

Dear Adilyn,

Oh, joy! Confide in her and I believe good things will follow. If she is the type of person who would be afraid to help, she isn't the type of person you would want to confide in any way. Keep that in mind. Just one person to talk to can make a considerable difference, and I pray that it will. Keep me informed of her whereabouts.

Love,
Your friend

April, 10th

Dear Friend,

A few hours have passed since the last letter I wrote. I couldn't help but have a shot or two, numbing myself from an overbearing guilty disgust over my actions of last night. Regardless of how much I needed to go through with them, the rain is still falling but had lightened up. I did go outside, down the creaking stairs at the end of the hallway and into the lobby.

I walked past the mirror I had never seen and pushed open the doors to find the man of the street sitting in his usual spot. I didn't want to stand over him and ask him to come inside; I thought that would make him feel inferior to me. He isn't. So, I sat down next to him. I tried talking to him, but he never seemed to understand what I was saying. He had an unfocused gleam in his eyes. He smiled when I talked, but I could tell he didn't really understand what was happening.

I noticed him shivering from the wet breezes that passed over his poor, heaving body. I went upstairs and picked a thick coat out of my closet. He wore it like a blanket, not a coat. I figured it was doing its job either way. I stood up and reached out my hand, ready to lead him upstairs, but he never took it. He just gave me another silent, dazed smile and then leaned back his head on the wall to rest. From here, I just let him be.

I began to walk a little way down to the record store. I stumbled when I walked. One or two had really been three or four. I stopped, embarrassed at myself. I looked down the street and, to my delight, the light in the top window of the store was on! I figured I better go see her tomorrow in a more decent state. But my joy for the return of my friend is immeasurable.

I am sitting in bed now, finishing this letter. My record is spinning me into sleep, where I ought to wake up to a little less gloomy, a little less lonely day.

Best regards,
Adilyn

April, 10th

Dear Friend,

There are people in this world who are completely gone. The average person would sneer or stare, but not you. For this, you are special. I am happy that you didn't go to the store intoxicated. I feel as though that would have left a horrible impression. Especially considering you have decided to let your walls down so that the sweet woman can try to mend your broken soul. I wish you joy, sweet girl.

Love,
Adilyn

April, 11th

Dear Loneliness,

It's almost as if you can sense your hold on me was loosening. I found a companion in that old woman, and it nearly killed you. And then, when she was gone, you gave it everything you had to try and kill me. I wonder if every moment I spend away from you increases how deeply I fall back when I return. But what if I never did fall back? What a dream that would be. Everyone is lonely sometimes. But I have done my time in your cell —enough for a few lifetimes. And I shall spend the rest of my time avoiding a return.

Adilyn

April, 11th

Dear Adilyn,

Nearly killed me? Have you forgotten about all the times someone came into your life just for you to squander the opportunity at a relationship with someone? And look at you now, deciding to tell a woman you just met all of the darker sides to your story. What a foolish girl. You shall soon learn that what nearly kills is never the same as what kills.

Love,
Loneliness

April, 11th

Dear Friend,

I am getting dressed and ready to make my walk down to the record store to meet the old lady. Albeit uninvited, I'm sure she would be glad to see me again, based on how she spoke to me during our last interactions. I am unsure if today will be the day that I ease into my confiding. But it will be soon.

Yours,
Adilyn

April, 11th

Dear Adilyn,

Regardless of whether it is now or in a few days' time, the important aspect of the situation is that you are taking advantage of the chance to speak to this woman about the things that you have kept hidden for so long.

Write to me soon.

Love,
Your friend

April, 11th

Dear Sweet woman,

Delight flooded through me when I saw you standing on the sidewalk in front of your store, smiling at me. Almost as if you knew I was coming. Almost as if you were waiting. I was so content in your store, talking with you again. You told me of your travels to see your grandson. It enthralled me to hear about him, to hear you letting me into your life and talking about things that you wouldn't just tell a stranger on the street.

And then I was astounded by what you told me next. You were talking to him about me! It made me feel a little hypocritical to be so shocked at this news. Our new friendship had been on my mind for the whole time we did not visit each other. But to talk about me? And then you went on to inform me that he is coming to see you soon. I said I would very much like to meet him, and you said you very much would like that too.

As this conversation went on, the rain outside seemed to soften. My chronic loneliness had, for the moment, all but subsided. What a feeling that was. How glad I am to have met you.

All of my best,
Adilyn

April, 11th

Dear Adilyn,

The rain has seemed to soften every day since our first meeting. I was standing outside wishing for a little sunlight, and then there you were! I did feel it coming. My grandson is coming soon, and I cannot say I am not thrilled! I would love for you to meet him, dear. And soon you will!

Love,
Sweet woman

April, 11th

Dear Friend,

Having lived for so long without anything to trigger an emotional response, I was not used to having to contain it. With that being said, I still think I did quite a satisfactory job in terms of maintaining my outright excitement throughout the duration of my conversation with the sweet woman. She has filled me with joy once again—my friendship with her. We are meeting

tomorrow morning for coffee again at the shop. I think
that in that setting, it will be easier to let myself open up
to her. Tell her the things I am going through. I will let
you know how that goes afterward.

Best regards,
Adilyn

April, 11th

Dear Adilyn,

Your friend is back! What a time this is becoming for
you! I am stuck with my awaiting to hear all about this
grandson of hers'. Do you know why he is coming? Just
to visit, perhaps, or will he stay awhile? Never mind that.
I am sure you are perfectly content with meeting yet
another important person in such little time. I hope all
goes well tomorrow. Do not be afraid. Open up to her.
You never have to tell her everything that you have gone
through. You may simply just ask for help. Subtly or not,
I am sure she would be willing to give some. Buildings
can sway in the hardest of winds; sometimes, another
building built in the way can block some of it.

Love,
Your friend

April, 12th

Dear Sweet woman,

The nervousness for today is palpable as I straighten myself up for our outing today. Truth be told, I didn't have my nightmare last night. Probably because I couldn't fall asleep for a long enough period of time to be at rest long enough to have a dream of any kind. The rain still falls outside but it seems to barely be a sound. Soft raindrops tap on my window this morning, providing no threat to the likes of my record player in the corner. What a peaceful morning this is turning out to be. I will see you soon.

Adilyn

April, 12th

Dear Adilyn,

What I saw and listened to today broke my heart. It was a little surprising to hear you tell me these things. I haven't known you long, and I figured you would take a little more time to let me in. But I have felt like you would. I watched these past weeks as you grasped the opportunity for a friend like you had been starving for one. I realized quickly after meeting you that you did certain little things within your mannerisms that made me think there could be some deeper issues lying underneath. You have been quick to change the subject when it falls on you; you never fixed your hair in front of me, and your eyes have a habit of finding the laces of your shoes instead of meeting mine.

I believe that I have become more than a friend to you today. Maybe I already was, and you were just building the courage to bring me closer. I became a rock of some kind, a solid structure that you could confide in. I fear you have had few to none. You told me about the things you do when you are alone and the way you think. You shared some of the memories that keep you lying awake when the moonlight reaches its peak. You spoke of a mirror in your lobby and of the hideous thing that lies idle beyond the door to your closet. You hurled these at me, and I graciously tried to catch each and every one of them.

It pained me to watch you sit there with a few soft tears sliding down your cheek. It pained me, but I fear that without the pain I felt in my heart today, yours might not be beating much longer. You looked lost telling me these things like a light was cast upon a very dark place in your soul. It didn't feel like we were casually sipping coffee anymore; it felt like something beautiful.

You may not think so, but now I have a space where I am able to aid you with the advice of a wise, wise woman. My advice to you, sweet child, is that all these things that haunt you will continue if you let them. Remove the fear from these things. Remove the anger and the hate, and you will only see events that didn't break you rather than events that still are. You are here with me, my child. I can see your face; I have seen you smile. They have not won. They are still interlocked in a battle within your mind. The things that scream at you to do horrible things have yet to scream loud enough because you are too strong. Once you silence them for good, they will not scream. Your mind can rest. And darling, your mind certainly needs some rest.

Love,
Sweet woman

April, 12th

Dear Friend,

My shadows can only walk as far as I let them. Engulfed in shadow, all I could see was shadow. Then, a thousand golden rays of sunlight pierced through the clouds. Shrinking my shadow. I am on top of it now. I sat with her and wept as I told her all my troubles. The rain had poured for so long I thought I was close to drowning. I let the floodgates open. Her weathered and beautiful face did not flinch at the horrors. She sat there, calm. Hanging onto my words as nobody ever had. She let me pour onto her. She offered her guidance. Simple guidance. To face it all, I must be able to speak softly to it. Confront it on my own. I shall start tonight. I am afraid of these things, but I am no longer idle lonesome in my fears.

Yours truly,
Adilyn

April, 12th

Dear Adilyn,

I knew that this woman would bring good things into your life—a little noise for the silence and some light for the dark. I am happy to hear you have decided to heed her advice. Grab the hand that will lead you out of the dark, my friend. Then you shall find your peace.

Love,
Your friend

April, 12th

Dear Monster,

Every now and then, you cross my mind. Not intentionally, of course. Usually, when I happen to glance at my reflection, I think of myself as hideous. But never as hideous as the night you sank your claws into me. I used to become paralyzed by your memory. I screamed out to nobody for help long after you left me in need of some. How naive I was back then. How handsome you were.

What was it we were supposed to do that night? Who am I kidding? I could tell you what phase the moon was in. I was so dressed up, Monster! Nobody had ever taken me on a date before. Nobody had ever shown me the gilded sinister twinkle of an eye. And I fell for it! Do you remember how I screamed? Oh, that laugh you had—taunting me. I fought and fought as hard as I could, obviously, to no avail. You were always going to be too strong. I felt you inside of me, robbing me. What a pretty dress I had on, Monster. Did you even notice? How did I do my hair? The necklace you left in pieces? Did you notice?

And then you took me back home like nothing had happened. Who could I tell? Who would believe me? Who would care even if they did? Oh, Monster, I spent forever trying to wash you off of me. I could feel you under my nails. I couldn't sleep, I couldn't eat. I just wanted a date, Monster. I see you around, but it's never you—just someone who looks the part. I stop in fear when I see them.

Oh, Monster, you broke me. You destroyed me. But my fear begins to reside, and anger will swell up in its place. These are not my final thoughts for you. This is the start

53

of my change. For your claws are beginning to slip out, years after you ripped them out yourself.

Wishing you only death
Adilyn

April, 13th

Dear Adilyn,

Ah, what a night that was. I had to think hard to remember it, but I do now. I ponder the idea that you have had a brewing hatred for me and for what happened that evening. I gave you everything you wanted that night. Why do you think I was out with you? With *you*? Almost comical that you think I had intended on truly giving you a date.

What would our peers at school think had they seen us together? I'd imagine they wouldn't believe it. I'd imagine you knew of this disbelief that they would have, and so you didn't tell a soul about it. Am I right? Or did you not tell a soul because you had gotten what you were after?

And now, have you strung a web of lies to act as though what happened was bad? Or was it really the best night of this filthy life you live?

Either way, you gave me what I wanted, and I know I had done the same. You can try and whisk the thought of me away, you filth, but I will remain in your head and under your dirty nails.

Love,
Monster

April, 13th

Dear Sweet woman,

There are still things that I didn't tell you during our little chat at the coffee shop.

In just the short time that I have known you, I felt that they would be overbearing to hear. I told you the basis of my troubles, and you provided me with the first steps to take to overcome them. You made me realize I was always able to face these things on my own; I just needed to push in the right direction. You gave me this push.

Last night, I started. I wrote to one of the evilest forces in my life: a thing, a monster who has terrorized me long during and after its act of torture. I never told you about that.

I am excited to come down and see you today. The rain is noticeably absent this morning. Clouds still dominate the sky, but somehow, they look less gloomy. I will see you soon.

Yours,
Adilyn

April, 13th

Dear Adilyn,

I feel there is more beneath your surface, sweet girl, but I shall not pry. I am the ears that will listen to you. You will only hear my words when you ask for them. I believe if you continue to face these entities, they will fade. They will fade into the darkness where you have dwelled as you are released from their captivity. The only thing I ask of you, sweet girl, is to continue the demonstration of strength that you have shown this cold world for so long. The voices will quiet as long as you keep silencing them.

Love,
Sweet woman

April, 13th

Dear Silence,

I know you will prevail over me one day. But how you must tremble to see that day is looking all the more distant than just a short time ago. I am getting louder. I know you will not break, but I will bend you further than I ever have. Beginning to feel a want to escape your grasp instead of a yearning to fall into it.

Adilyn

April, 13th

Dear Adilyn,

You are losing a valuable companion, but you don't seem to think so. Why would you want to even exist in a place like this? Death is an incredible thing, dear girl. You won't be remembered long after you are gone. Eventually, nobody will be. I give you a place to think, to remember how cold this world has treated you. You have spent your life begging for any type of warmth. A friend, some family, love, you have even begged for just a short break from the rain. And truly, you have received none of it. So, I aid your remembrance. I aid these thoughts that you run from. The ones that could make the horrors vanish. You cannot escape them. They breathe so long as you breathe. Quiet down, sad girl, stay quiet and remember it all.

Love,
Silence

April, 13th

Dear Man of the street,

I passed you again today, as I do every time I leave my building. Your face swelled with joy at the sight of me and the food I brought down to give to you.

I won't try to invite you up again after last time. It seems to be here where you are comfortable. Here, where the people fear. The people frown, but to you, it's home. You sleep here three floors beneath me at the bottom of this three-floor building.

We both see the cherry blossom every night before we drift into sleep. The shutter over the entrance blocks the rain from you the way my window blocks it for me.

I wonder about your silence. Is it the noises of the city that work the way my record player does? Can you hear your silence? Can you escape it? Is it evil and alluring for you as well? I am being dragged away from mine after

so long of dwelling in it. I wonder if you would want to
be dragged away from yours.

Yours,
Adilyn

April, 13th

Dear Adilyn,

Kind girl, nobody ever really gives me a passing glance
as I sit in my spot. Not that I really mind. I have
nothing, but to actually have nothing means you have
nothing to weep about. Nothing to worry about.
Nothing to love, yes, but nothing to hate. My record
player, kind girl, is my eyes opening in the morning. It is
the air that fills my lungs. My silence is friendly, and I
wrap myself in it and think of the good of my past. Not
the evil. Why spend time drowning in silence when you
could float upon it? It is a lethal thing, but it is also a
thing of beauty. I do appreciate your generosity. I cannot
show it to you very well, but I do see you.

Love,
Man of the street

April, 13th

Dear Sweet woman,

Your grandson is coming so very soon! You seemed
thrilled talking about him, and that made me glad. You
told me he will be here in two days and time, and you

need to spend tomorrow setting up his staying space in your little home on top of the record store. I offered my help, and you seemed gracious enough to accept it.

You asked me if I had started the process of dealing with my past and smiled when I told you I had. We sat and watched the street artist set up her stuff for the day. She gleamed as she did it. I gazed at her, admiring the profession she seemed to enjoy. Wincing at the thought that I, too, will be making money tonight.

The clouds covered the scene on the street, but no rain fell. How refreshing that was. We parted ways, and I said I'd be over mid-morning tomorrow. I will see you then.

My best,
Adilyn

April, 13th

Dear Adilyn,

She certainly does love what she does, that street artist. And how could she not? Brightening the moods of so many has clearly left hers' bright as well. I am glad that you offered to come over and help me move tomorrow.

I fear I am getting far too weak to do that kind of heavy lifting on my own. It is lovely, the absence of rain. It had fallen far too long and hard for any type of person to dance in it. I will see you soon.

Love,
Sweet woman

April, 13th

Dear Friend,

I long for tomorrow, but I will have to make it through tonight first. I have had much worse nights to get through, but my scheduled meetings with the sweet woman have made these recent nights feel especially long. Something to look forward to often makes the dull even duller.

My record is spinning and not fighting any rain, but it will have to be loud enough to soothe me once he arrives. Before he does, I will continue to take the advice of my friend. I will reach a little further back, someplace dark, but someplace that I need to face in order to find myself again.

I know the dream will come back, but I feel I am beginning to torment it for once.

Regards,
Adilyn

April, 13th

Dear Adilyn,

I despise this work that you do. And you know it causes these dreams, yet you continue to do so!

I hate asking things of you, dear friend, but you must stop! I sigh now because I know you won't stop despite my constant protests.

I will say I am proud of you for continuing to slay the old beasts of memory that roam in your silence.

I am here if you need me. Always.

Love,
Your friend

April, 13th

Dear School,

A religious school for children. How pathetic. Whose idea was it to force ideas down the throats of the youth? With no life experience to mold them into making decisions that they will carry out throughout the duration of their lives? Ludicrous. How I loathed that school. I wonder about the moral state of those involved. Is religion supposed to be about belief? Isn't it about faith? How is someone going to get a false power trip so disgustingly strong that they decide they have control over what another person believes? And for it to be children—of course, it will be children. Such easy targets, right? Such a malleable mind.

I vividly remember the chair. Oh, the chair. Once a week, each student was required to meet with the man in the chair opposite. We stood single file, awaiting our turn into the room. My stomach would squirm. My hands would shake. My mind raced to come up with another lie to tell the man. Another false confession. They would want a confession out of me after I spent the night wide awake, hoping with all I had that my father wouldn't find me after his pours. How was I to come up with one? What kind of life is that for a child to live? Thinking of it makes my hands shake as I pen this letter.

As I drift away, though, further and further from that time, I start to lose my resentment. School, you cannot control me now. You never did.

Adilyn

April, 13th

Dear Adilyn,

You really were always a vile young lady. Ungrateful and untrusting, the audacity of you to step outside the lines that we drew for you. You must have forgotten that the rules we put in place for you were always for your own good. But you were always too much of a brat even to care. You never showed any faith in God; you never even seemed to respect our teachings. You never belonged in his kingdom anyway.

You ought to be burnt in hell like all the rest who don't believe. Like all the rest who would dare lie in the chair next to our priest. The church never targeted you in any kind of way, foolish girl. We just knew what was best for you. We hold the good word, so why would you truly believe your ideas matter if they are different than ours?

You are wrong. You are shameful to his throne. You shall be punished for eternity, filth. And you will beg for the mercy of the hand you turned away from your whole life.

Love,
School

April, 14th

Dear Friend,

Another morning with no sunshine. I am beginning to get the feeling that these clouds are temporary. Just about as temporary as the sour mood I awoke to. I felt dirty because of what I had done. Awfully. I stood up and walked about my small room for a minute or two. Unable to see my reflection anywhere. Not want to anyways.

I didn't stare long at my closet the way I normally do. I didn't think about what was inside. If I don't open the door, it will only exist in my dreams. My negative mood did surrender, however, when I remembered the plans for the day. I don't really know much about the sweet woman's grandson. Only that he is coming; I will be off soon. Off to take my mind away.

I moved swiftly as I got dressed. I grabbed a few of the dollars I had made the night before and stuffed them into my pocket. I considered giving them to the man of the street but decided they were better spent if I spent them on something for him rather than just handing them over. I am leaving now to go to the house on top of the record store. I will be writing soon.

All of my best,
Adilyn

April, 14th

Dear Adilyn,

You continue never to acknowledge my thoughts on your line of work, so I shall cease to give them. I have repeated it enough for you to disregard my words with utterly no shame clearly. I do have a sneaking feeling, however, that you know I am right. You already know how obvious it is that what you are doing is killing you. But I digress. I want to hear all about your meeting with the sweet woman's grandson in the coming days when it happens. I hope it goes over well. I am sure the man will indeed appreciate your generosity. Keep being kind. Keep staying true to yourself and your heart, lovely girl, and good things will follow.

Love,
Your friend

April, 14th

Dear Man of the street,

I sometimes wonder why you picked my building of all buildings to lean upon and make into your home. Why not someplace nicer? Why not in a place where people have money to spare? You chose a very sad street to settle on—a place where hope glimmers but hardly ever shines through. People feed off hope here. Even though there isn't much of it, it is what keeps many going. It's what keeps me going.

I walked down to the shop halfway between the record store and my building, next to the coffee spot where the painter paints. I bought you some food and then walked back to give it to you. I got another wispy smile from you. Seemingly all you could muster.

However, creating a smile on another's face is something I hold in very high regard. It's an easy thing to do, but few people find it important. Or as important as I do. I fear most of the world is comfortable with a frown.

I fear it's all they've ever known. Worse, comfortable with a blank face. No reason to frown, never a reason to smile. Just numb to sadness and a stranger to delight. It doesn't mean they are too far gone. They could regain their feelings just as I do. What a dream it is starting to become. Rather than the nightmare I would wake up from just to wake up to.

Sincerely,
Adilyn

April, 14th

Dear Adilyn,

Dear child, in my old age, you tend to stop needing worldly things to be happy. I have lived my life. I have seen it all. I sit here with no plans, no reason either. It is just the place my path has taken me. Maybe to sit around and see a miracle. Maybe I have earned something like that.

Love,
Man of the street

April, 14th

Dear Sweet woman,

We were busy today, too busy to talk about my second letter that was written last night. I didn't mind. I know these are problems I must face on my own. I am just glad to have a person with whom I can share my thoughts when the mood strikes. We worked from the morning into the evening hours until the sun dipped beyond the clouds still dominant over the sky. Hiding the orange and pink rays of another missed sunset from illustrating the street we call home.

I was intrigued to see the place you lived in, for I had only ever been downstairs in the store. It was similar to mine. Small, with a single bathroom. There were two rooms, though, which were different from my place. I learned nobody had inhabited that room since your late husband. And you couldn't bear to go inside and straighten it up. You said that is why you graciously accepted my offer to help. You said you needed me to push you to go in and clean. You said you needed me.

A window on the far side of the room opened to the street. We left it open in hopes of breezes to float in and cool us off. If you stand by the window, you can see the coffee spot, the artist doing her work, and the little store where I bought a warm meal for the man of the street on this cloudy day. If you open it, though, and lean your head out a little, you can see my building—the man of the street, the cherry blossom, and my window. The room was dusty, having not been used in so long. Dimly lit as well. We cleaned and brightened it up quite a bit. The bed was still made from the last time it was slept.

We changed the sheets anyway with some fresh ones you kept in your closet.

Your grandson arrives tomorrow evening. You said we should have coffee in the morning and then plan to meet later on so that I can meet him. This made the joy swell inside me once again. You have a habit of creating this feeling for me despite it being lost for so many years. I left an hour or so after the sun went down and night fell on our street. I walked past the man of the street, now asleep, not looking at the mirror as I walked inside my building, up my stairs, and into my room. Happy having spent the day with you. Happy to not have him come tonight. Happy.

Until tomorrow,
Adilyn

April, 14th

Dear Adilyn,

You and your help today was quite a blessing. I was happy to show you around and the place where I live. I appreciate your kindness, sweet girl. Thank you.

Love,
Sweet woman

April, 14th

Dear Friend,

Although the day has worn me, I will still write tonight. I will confront my past once again. I will stare at it. Talk to it, even though I have shuddered at the memories for so long. Wincing at the thoughts in my own head as I remember them. Blocking them out to avoid the feeling they gave me then. But I cannot hide from them, for they still rule over me from the deepest shadows of my mind. A reinvention of myself cannot occur if I cannot face the things that have made me who I am. I must tear down the old to build the new.

Wishing the best,
Adilyn

April, 14th

Dear Adilyn,

Your strength is admirable. I do believe I know what you will write to tonight. You are strong. You are brave. Many could not face what you will in the coming minutes. Many die trying. Be well, dear friend.

Love,
Your friend

April, 14th

Dear Attempt,

It gets hard to tell when the night falls here because of the clouds that blanket the sky. But it wasn't hard to tell that night. In fact, I waited all day. Hidden in my room, following the path of the sunlight as the shadow slowly spun around the tree in my yard. I wasn't scared. I was ready. I was not sad about what I was going to do. I felt that it would make everything better. I felt as if the people in my life would be better off. I didn't have many friends, but the people I did interact with always seemed to be brought down by my presence. And who was I to put that burden upon them?

I sat in the bedroom of my childhood home. Nobody else was there. My father was at work, and my mother just tended to disappear sometimes for a while. It didn't matter that they were gone. They were going to be asleep when I did it anyway. I remember sitting in that room. Waiting. I had a plan; it was a good plan, too. My school bag was leaned up against my peeling gray wall. I sat on my twin bed and stared at it for hours. I had spent the day before down by the pond collecting rocks. I filled the bag with rocks and struggled as I lugged it back to my room. It sat there in the darkest corner of my room. Heavy and perfect. I also had a belt. Strung up on my closet rail. Those two things were all that I needed.

The sun came down especially fast that day. Daring me to go with it. Once it went down, I was totally numb. I grabbed my bag and my belt and shakily undid the latch that kept my window locked. My sweaty hand pushed on the panes, allowing it to swing open, and then I was out. It was especially dark that night. Even though the skies were clear, it was loud, too. An eerie sort of loud. A cacophony of birds and crickets and all the other creatures of the night. Silence was absent as it allured me to drown in it. As if it was mercifully giving me one last explosion of sound before I was engulfed in its cave. Loneliness was present, and it pushed my feet forward—one step after the other. There were screams for me to stop, but never any loud enough to care. Never any loud enough to let me know they cared.

When I got to the pond, I looked up into the night sky. The stars didn't seem to twinkle that night. The plants looked wilted. The air seemed stale. I hoisted the bag onto my shoulders and then synched the belt around my stomach. I took a few more steps towards the bank. The backpack only added a few pounds to the already seemingly millions that weighed on me. The silence smirked. The loneliness curved its lips in an evil leer. The words and the images in my head rang out like the choir of a thousand broken souls.

I turned around. Walked backward until I couldn't touch anymore, and then I leaned back and let the weight of the rocks pull me into my silent ending. But as I sank, the flaw in my plan was realized. The fast sinking and strong pull of the rocks down into the water loosened the clasp of my belt. I was only halfway down before it came undone. Suddenly, I was thrust back into the world I had just said goodbye to. The world I didn't belong in. I regretted none of it. I dove down for my bag, but it was so dark I couldn't see a thing. I swam up to the surface and then to the edge, where the animals had since ended their symphony. I sat there and cried. Sobbed. Silent sobs. Lonely sobs. This wasn't my only failure, but it was the first. I was so confident. So sure of what I was doing. A feeling I never had before and I haven't had since.

70

This night is beginning not to encapsulate my mind so much these days of recent. I believe it is the basis of my dream. The catalyst of my nightmare. But it is starting to fade, and for that, I cannot express my joy; I do not have any words worthy of it. Attempt, you are beginning to be a reminder of when I was weaker. But that is okay because to have been weaker then means that I am stronger now.

Making you fade away,
Adilyn

April, 14th

Dear Adilyn,

What you attempted to accomplish that night by the pond would have been a great thing. People try every day to find out why; well, some reasons are understandable, and other reasons are created entirely in the mind of sadness's beholder. The reasons as to why you tried that night and why you tried a myriad of other times were perfectly reasonable. How could you take all that pressure put upon you? All the things you were forced to go through at such young ages. And nobody really noticed. I am not weakening now. You are just forcing your mind onto some false hope that things are starting to brighten up. They aren't. But it doesn't matter, for you know the taste of the sweetest escape. You are addicted to it, and I am the one who put it on your tongue.

Love,
Attempt

April, 15th

Dear Friend,

A morning where I am able to wake without reeling from the disheartening effects of that nightmare is always a good morning. I figured I would've because of how much I thought about my attempt last night before I slept. Yet, this morning, I woke up peacefully. Again, no rain, not even a drizzle. The clouds seemed to dissipate last night as well. Not quite a day of sunshine, but much better than what our street has seen recently. Again, I get dressed and prepare to get coffee with my friend, the sweet woman. What a day this could be! I will be in touch.

Yours truly,
Adilyn

April, 15th

Dear Adilyn,

When these clouds finally do move to make way for the smile of the sun, I hope you will find it in yourself to smile back. Write soon.

Love,
Your friend

April, 15th

Dear Loneliness,

Silence is inevitable, but it is easier to hold off at any moment than you are. It will have me in the end, but I could always escape it for the time being. You, however, are harder to be released from. Company isn't hard to come across, but a company where you are cared for and heard can be very difficult to find. It takes time to build relationships like that. Sometimes, it just takes luck. But once you have this company, it takes more to lose it. A record player can fall on the floor and break. A true friend takes much more.

Adilyn

April, 15th

Dear Adilyn,

A suggestion that a company is difficult to lose is an absurd one. All the good you have going for you can vanish in a blink of an eye. It will vanish before you know it. You should know this just as well as anybody. And then you will come back to me, lonely girl. When it is gone, I will be your only company yet again. I will be waiting. I always am.

Love,
Loneliness

April, 15th

Dear Sweet woman,

Oh, I could see that smile from a mile away. Not that I had to walk a mile, but it lit up the street like one of the painter's customers. You would think there wasn't a cloud in the sky by the way you sat there grinning. I knew not to flatter myself with the disillusion that I was all of the reason for this smile. Although I was quietly satisfied knowing I was part of it. I know you're excited to see your grandson tonight. This was confirmed by the way you talked about him. The stories you told me about his childhood. Raising him in the absence of his parents with the help of your late husband before you moved to the city. I am excited, too. It still blows me away how my fortunes seemed to change and how one friendship was able to change a few perceptions that I had of the world. Ones that continued to drag me down further every day.

Further and further as they could never be satisfied. For these changes, I am thankful and proud. I wrote again last night. It was freeing. I am not sure if I didn't have my dream or if I just didn't remember it. Either way, I am glad I didn't wake up to those images in my mind. I will see you tonight.

Your friend,
Adilyn

April, 15th

Dear Adilyn,

My beautiful girl, you know you always bring a smile to my face.

In fact, between our newfound friendship and the news of my grandson coming to town, I haven't smiled this much in ages. Tonight will be a blissful experience for us all. I am excited about it.

See you then!

April, 15th

Dear Friend,

I have a few hours before I am supposed to be upstairs in the sweet woman's apartment above the record store where I met her—only a few hours until I meet her grandson. I feel my stomach in knots. I don't really have anything nice to wear for the occasion. Maybe that will be fine. If he's anything like her, then I hardly think he'll mind. She is very accepting of me being myself. I pace around my room.

Filthy habits that I learned from my parents are the only way I know how to deal with anxiety like this. My bottle of gin sits idle from where I left it during the sweet woman's absence. I will not succumb to these methods today. I refuse. Anxious thoughts have ruined me before. They have kept me away from putting myself out there from being myself at all. I won't let it stop me today.

Maybe I'll write to pass the time. Maybe I should write

about these feelings. They are just as destructive as the evils I have written to the past few nights.

Regards,
Adilyn

April, 15th

Dear Adilyn,

I plead you not to fret yourself too hard about this evening. It is just a gathering of friends. The anxiety you feel is grossly unwarranted. Think of how comfortable you are speaking to the sweet woman. So comfortable that you willingly told her things that have never escaped your lips for another. I want to hear all about tonight once you are home. I will be here waiting.

Love,
Your friend

April, 15th

Dear Anxiety,

You have a way of twisting perceptions of the world. How is it that you can turn a group of people who won't notice a small flaw into the harshest critics alive? How can you make me feel that everyone is judging me all the time? And probably making them feel as if they were being judged all the time.

A powerful thing, you could make a person go delusional with fear—a potent evil with the potential to ruin the strongest confidence. And if you could ruin someone with strong confidence, it's easy to see how you have been able to have your way with me for so long.

Unfair comparisons to others. Unfair, inhuman standards that I have brought upon myself. Let me be!

The way I've fought you is also destructive. Drinking until I am incapable of thinking just to rid myself of you.

The thing, though, anxiety, is that I know you are wrong. I know you are just in my head. I still work to combat you, but not in the ways that I have been.

You may never be beaten, but you will be reduced.

Your victim,
Adilyn

April, 15th

Dear Adilyn,

Your arrogance is truly baffling, unwanted girl. Do you really think people pass you by and think nothing of you? You are the perfect image to make another person feel better about themselves. By comparing themselves to wretches, they have to feel good. It is a comparison nobody can lose against.

You feel so invisible all the time, but you know they are staring at you. Sneering at you. You know they are judging you, right?

Go ahead and wash me away again with that bottle since it seems to be the only way you know how. Surely, your new friend and her grandson wouldn't be surprised if you showed up drunk. Would anyone?

Go ahead and put on the finest outfit you have. Surely, you couldn't make even that look awful. Right? Prove me wrong since you want to so bad.

I own you. I always have. You will bow to my hand whenever the mood strikes me to make you. You always have.

Love,
Anxiety

April, 15th

Dear Mirror,

I stroll past once again, never even offering a glance. I won't lie to you and say that I came close, but this is the only time turning my head to face you has ever crossed my mind. I don't wear fancy clothes, but I did the best with what I could. I brushed my long black hair, the same color as my outfit. I wore my only necklace, a gold-plated chain with a small sapphire stone, the same color as my eyes, placed in the center. It will take more to give you a look. I am not there yet.

Sincerely,
Adilyn

April, 15th

Dear Adilyn,

You bore me, sad girl. You and your insufferable lack of confidence. Could you find beauty in your reflection? Maybe. But you don't even dare to try. I hang from this wall, knowing you will never see me. How many more times will you pass by? How much more can you stand the fear of seeing your face? It must be hard. But it must be harder to see something shattered in glass that has never been chipped.

Love,
Mirror

April, 15th

Dear Sweet woman,

The common area for guests in your little apartment may have been the birthplace of yet another turning point in my life. You can tell that you raised your grandson. He has the same proper poise and gentle demeanor that you boast. He speaks with the same silver tongue of enthrallment. Telling stories with the same enthusiasm as you. I didn't want to ask how long he was going to be staying with you. I felt that it might possibly be an insensitive question, being that I don't really know why he is here in the first place. That was never mentioned. It's exciting that he intends to help you work the shop as gratitude for him staying with you. I figure that was probably his idea because you are the type to give and expect nothing in return. I thanked you both for letting me share the enjoyment of his arrival, and I got up to leave. He stood up as well. I didn't know why, maybe trying to be respectful and acknowledge my departure? And then he asked to walk me out. I said it was okay, but he insisted.

We didn't talk much on the way back to my building, but it was still a comfortable silence. The safest I had ever felt on that street. We said goodbye on the threshold of my building. I wished him a safe walk back, he thanked me, spun around and disappeared into the night, beyond the illumination of the miscellaneous lights that leave patches of light across the street. There was a feeling that I hadn't felt in a very long time. If ever. I cannot even really describe it. But I am excited about the time I will have to spend with you both. I will see you soon.

Thank you,
Adilyn

April, 15th

Dear Adilyn,

The three of us sat there in my little room, and our eyes all twinkled as if a ray of sunlight had finally broken through these dreary clouds. I felt the world become a little less lonely this evening. I hope you did enjoy the time you spent with us. I know that I did.

Love,
Sweet woman

April, 15th

Dear Friend,

Oh my, what a pretty man. He bore features I had never seen—not like this. Green eyes with a fiery orange ring around his pupils. He towered over me with broad shoulders and a blonde, clean-cut middle-part haircut.

He seemed intelligent as well, telling stories as we sat with his grandmother. I had to remind myself to continue to listen to his words quite a few times. He also seemed genuinely interested in what I had to say. He asked me questions, and we talked about my relationship with the sweet woman.

I find it difficult to believe he could be interested in pursuing me romantically. However, I am still very content with his company alone, even if it is that of a platonic kind.

What a day it was! My record player will spin as I drift away tonight. The clouds hang under the stars, but no rain falls from them. A quiet night. A comfortable silence.

Goodnight, my friend,
Adilyn

April, 15th

Dear Adilyn,

Well, you certainly sound enthralled by him. I find your romanticizing of this man odd after all that you have been through. Maybe he will be different, just as your friendship with the sweet woman seems different. I do advise caution; however, I don't think that you will be able to endure any more aches in your already worn heart. From what you have said, you seem to be okay with nothing more than a friendship. I think that is a good thing. A safe thing. Goodnight, sweet girl.

Love,
Your friend

April, 16th

Dear Silence,

The situational dependence you require is so fascinating to me. I spend so much of my time trying to avoid you. Avoiding you keeps me from stepping too far into the depths of my mind. But, sometimes, you are a lovely thing. A venue to breathe in a way. An enabler of self-peace. Loneliness with silence is what I fear. Silence on its own, when you are not so lonesome, can be quite divine. Silence, you have never bowed so low to me. I have never controlled my silence like I have the days of recent. It appears now that I may have added a second voice to my arsenal against you. For now, I am loud.

Keep bending,
Adilyn

April, 16th

Dear Adilyn,

I have always tried to convince you that you need me, quiet girl. I am only as evil as you make me out to be. But isn't it nice to have a space to collect yourself? Your loneliness has been what has made me seem so cruel, but I am not. Fall into me, mold me into your tool rather than your mind's weapon against its own host. And then you will appreciate me.

Love,
Silence

April, 16th

Dear Artist,

As I sat alone at the coffee shop this morning, waiting for my friend, I watched you. I admired your jovial mood as you set up your workstation. I couldn't help but compare it to the way I set up my own.

You set up your canvas with a beaming smile. I close my blinds to hide from the rest of the world. You carefully check the colors on your palette. I turn my record player up as a way to escape the situation I feel forced to put myself through. You sharpen your charcoal. I dull my mind with the bottle.

You work during the day. I work in the dead of the night. You want the world to watch you work. I am too embarrassed by mine to want even to believe it happened. The sight of your joy inspires and nauseates me. But you helped me realize something today.

I cannot go on with the work that I do, Artist. It is as simple as that. It rips me apart. Shreds all the fractions of self-esteem that I could possibly muster. The work is unhealthy; I cannot do it sober. I cannot go on with it.

My anxiety and my past have led me to the work that I do. When my sweet friend arrived and sat down next to me, I saw her as an opportunity, once again, to escape another sad part of my life. To ask for a favor such as the one I am thinking of might turn out poorly. It may be too big of a thing to ask of her. But I will. I don't exactly have a lot to lose.

Keep inspiring,
Adilyn

April, 16th

Dear Adilyn,

Child, would it kill you to come have a seat across from me? Would it be such a horrible thing to spend a minute or two in my chair? Do you see my smile? Do you see the smile of others? Do you really think they think perfection of themselves? They come to me to get what they hope to see when they look in a mirror. It is not false hope I give them; it is the realization of possibility. They could see themselves in their perfect image, and I could give you the same feeling! Come sit with me, sweet girl. Come soon.

Love,
Artist

April, 16th

Dear Sweet woman,

Today, as we chatted and drank our coffee, I impulsively asked a favor. A favor I realized I needed just moments before you sat down. I asked for a job at your record store. You smiled at me with that endearing, wise smile that you have, and you said, "By all means." Had it really been that simple this entire time? Could I have just asked that question almost two weeks ago instead of putting myself through those horrible nights? No matter. You are the one who made me realize I must conquer my past rather than dwell on it. You even said I could start tomorrow. I will be there in the morning to start. I will see you then.

April, 16th

Dear Adilyn,

I was wondering how long it was going to take you to ask if you could come work at the shop. I was a little disappointed that you hadn't already. I am getting older, and the news of my grandson coming to help was quite incredible. Now, with another person to help, it seems that a hefty load is about to be taken off of my back. How fortunate I am! My grandson was excited to hear the news as well. Tomorrow, we will begin our work together!

Love,
Sweet woman

April, 16th

Dear Friend,

I feel as if an enormous weight has been lifted from my shoulders. One that was mentally and physically crushing for so long. But it has lifted. It is over. Newer and better things are coming. I couldn't fathom this kind of change mere weeks ago, but they are happening. Tomorrow is my first day. I will work with the sweet woman and her grandson at the store. I do not have much knowledge of record players, records, or even music in itself, but doing anything other than what I was doing is clearly progress. I will be writing soon.

Yours,
Adilyn

April, 16th

Dear Adilyn,

Could it really be true? Have you finally taken my advice and quit that horrible job of yours? I am sure you are thrilled to be working with the sweet old woman and her grandson. Even more so to relieve yourself of such detrimental work. Detrimental to your mental and physical health. Your happiness, self-esteem, and perspective on the world. Today, I am happy. Today, we rejoice.

Love,

Your friend

April, 16th

Dear Client,

You are not coming tonight. You will never come again. I sit on my bed and stare at my door. Thinking about the times, I would sit in disgust. Waiting for it to open and for him to come in. The mere thought formed a tear that slid down my cheek, the thought of never having to be near those filthy footsteps, of never having to watch that handle turn, of never having to rely on the sound of a record player to escape from where I was. The thought of not having to wake up disgusted and alone. To see dirty money lying on the counter of my dresser.

You held me down for so long, Client. How does it feel knowing I'm gone? Probably feels the same for you. At least for the ones who never slipped their wedding ring into their pocket before they came into my room. Never noticed the tan line around that finger. I was just as faceless to them as they were to me. Neither of us ever truly wanted to be there, and yet there we were. Committing the act that let guilt hang over us like the looming clouds that erase any sunshine.

But you never have to come back here. I never have to keep that door unlocked. Approach me on the street, and I shall walk away. More free than I have ever been. Now, I will lay on this bed that used to feel so wretched. The place where we performed our hidden dance. This bed shall be no more to me now than a place to sleep. I smile, knowing it will never be any less than that.

Good riddance,
Adilyn

April, 16th

Dear Adilyn,

You never meant much to me, or anyone probably. You aren't the only lowly filth running around this sad world. There will be another that will do what you did. There will be a thousand more. There is a family who waits for me at home. They will never even know your name. I will find another you.

Love,
Client

April, 17th

Dear Friend,

Two weeks ago, I wrote you a letter. I was lost, startled by a nightmare that left me in fear that I had completely lost myself. It was raining that day. Pouring. Not today. Something spectacular happened today. I woke up to sunshine. The first of it I had seen in a long time. The clouds resided, and the light burst into my room through my window. I wanted to dance in the rays. And I would've had I not needed to get myself ready to go down to the record store. The tune that echoes through my room this morning was one I had heard many times, but it seemed brighter today. I am leaving now. I will write to you once I am home.

Yours,
Adilyn

April, 17th

Dear Adilyn,

Ah, the sun has returned. Now, you can let this smile come out and paint your face. What good! I know that smile of yours is shy. It has been many times wiped right off of your face after it thought it was safe to come out. It has been broken, but that doesn't mean it cannot be fixed. Bring that smile out, pretty girl, and let it shine alongside this brand-new sunshine.

Love,
Your friend

April, 17th

Dear Man of the street,

I wonder how long it's been since the sun has come out for you. Do you see it as I do today? You gave me another foggy smile as I passed by today. Another reminder that all it takes is a glimmer of light to help someone find their way out of a cave.

Best wishes,
Adilyn

April, 17th

Dear Adilyn,

I knew the sun was here when I felt it over the wrinkled skin I wear. I could hear the bird's song from atop the building I lean against. I knew it was here when you came out of the door of the lobby, and I got a rare smile in return for one of my own.

Love,
Man of the street

April, 17th

Dear Artist,

I feel the smiles you cause are the drive for your work. I smiled because of you as I passed your stand. It was indirect, as we didn't interact. But knowing that I was on the way to do something in the sunlight rather than the shadows was enough to make a smile curve onto my face.

Thank you,
Adilyn

April, 17th

Dear Adilyn,

Don't think I didn't notice the grin as you passed by. I only love putting smiles on the faces of those who need one because it puts one on mine. I don't know where you are going, pretty girl, but you look happy to be on your way. And for that, I am glad.

Love,
Artist

April, 17th

Dear Sweet woman,

How happy I am to have the opportunity to come to work with you and your grandson in the store. I was in there for longer than I had ever been before, which led me to admire its quaint yet regal beauty. The first time I came here was to buy the record player and some records to go with it. The second time was to get it repaired, which led to the beginning of our blossoming friendship. All the other times I have been inside the store, I have been very focused on whatever conversation we were having, and I did not pay much attention to what was inside. It is a lovely store, a place where a mind can ease. A sweet smell, imitating that of a new book, flirts with the nose as you walk inside.

The store isn't very large. The wooden floor is polished and obviously frequently cleaned. The shelves on the walls are made of oak, discolored so that there are dark spots among them. There are record players on display on those shelves and more in a little closet that is shut off to customers. The ceiling hangs low, and lamps are set up around the building to illuminate the space. There is the counter where the sweet old lady sits. This is where she talks to the guests, shuffles through the records, collects the payments, and fixes any damaged record players just as she fixed mine. Her grandson sat at the desk with her today.

There was quite a plethora of records that had been damaged. I suppose I never really noticed how busy the store gets. People shuffled in and out all day, bringing back records that they had rented, purchasing new ones, and some just flicked through all the available records without ever buying one. I spent my day sweeping the floor after the bumbles of people would come in and out, tracking the dirt with them as they walked. I also organized the available records from the box—first by genre, and then, from there, I organized them alphabetically.

I admired all the records that were sitting out, dusted them, and then went into the back closet to try and find the same kind of record player that was sitting in the corner of my room right now. When I couldn't, I asked your grandson about my record player. He explained to me that almost every record player we sell is different— handcrafted, right here in the shop by his grandmother. He said that it was the fascination of his grandfather that led her into this business. He shared that his grandfather was fascinated with the structure of record players and was working on one when he met her in another little record store somewhere far off from here.

All of the players were pretty expensive, and I realized that the sweet woman had clearly given me a deal before we even became friends. I smiled upon realizing this.

The shop opens in the later part of the morning, so the sweet woman and I made plans to meet for coffee the next couple of mornings before we both go on into the shop. I was walked home again by her grandson, comforted in knowing that he would be the last company I have for the evening. Even though I secretly didn't want him to go once we got to my building, I thanked him again, and then, just as smoothly as last time, he spun around and walked off into the night.

See you tomorrow
Adilyn

April, 17th

Dear Adilyn,

To give you a place to come and be away from yourself for awhile is something I am proud of doing. You have given me a friendship and some much-needed help. An equal trade in my eyes, even if you hardly think so. I would expect that you wouldn't. My grandson is ecstatic about your presence. I believe something beautiful could blossom between the two of you, but I will stay out of that way. Thank you for coming here today, sweet child, I will see you tomorrow.

Love,
Sweet woman

April, 17th

Dear Record Player,

I should've known there was none other like you. The sentimental attachment for you makes your inanimate nature less noticeable. You fought for me. With me, rather. You still do. It feels silly to praise something with no life. Then again, you kept me treading the silence while it was whispering for me to drown in it. Your job tonight is to serenade the room that only I fill as I write again. Confronting my past, I stopped dwelling on it in the melodies that kept me in my room. Away from it all. The melodies brought by you.

Forever gracious
Adilyn

April, 17th

Dear Adilyn,

When silence whispers to you that everything is wrong, I will bring the voice that shouts that it is not. When your loneliness ices your heart, I am there to sing a song of love. When this world has all but turned your life upside down, you can follow my rhythm until you find yours again. Forever and always.

Love,
Record player

April, 17th

Dear Relative,

I'll call you relative because even though we are blood-related, we are not family. Today is the anniversary of your funeral. I will forget standing in the pews three rows back from the casket. Everyone was crying. Nobody knew. The stained-glass windows had the curtains drawn, so there was no sunlight lingering in the dim church. But what a sunny day it was. I saw some faces watching me out of the corner of my eye, seemingly appalled that I didn't seem to care. Nobody knew. They quickly turned away when I looked back at them. Afraid to confront my defiant nature, they just stood there quietly, sickened by my casual demeanor. Nobody knew.

But I knew. I knew I was a little girl once. I was just a child. You knew that, too; your black heart twisted. Twisted to the point where I doubt you even had one. You knew my house was not a home. I was just a child. Everyone knew that. You knew that sometimes it was so unstable that a child wouldn't be able to survive. Everyone knew that, too. You knew you should offer your residence to me when mine wasn't safe. Everyone praised you for that. That's all they ever saw. That's all they ever knew.

I didn't know how to stop you. I was just a child. And when you were done, once you were full of sick satisfaction, you would tell me not to tell a soul. And you knew I wouldn't. Who would believe me? I was just a child. And then you died. You were gone, and I didn't feel a thing. You died just for me to trust another monster. Nobody knew about him either. They might've believed me if I told them about him. But I was afraid they wouldn't because you convinced me that they wouldn't way back when I was just a child.

Rot in hell
Adilyn

April, 17th

Dear Adilyn,

Where could you run when a monster hides in plain sight? I had the similar wicked nature of another monster in your life, but your story about the other one is much more believable. Where do you hide if you live in the monsters' house? The same monster who so generously offered you a place to live while your immediate family went through troubling times. How saintly I looked doing that—just to prey on the defenseless.

It amused me, the little charade we put on together. How you silently screamed as loud as you could, hoping that anyone could hear you. But they wouldn't ever hear you, would they? They barely would let you get a word out. And if you did manage to speak, if someone did listen and did believe you, were they really going to do anything to stop it? How do you get away if you depend on the monster that is terrorizing you?

Did it hurt knowing you wouldn't have a bed to sleep in if you ran away? Even though you were too afraid to fall asleep most nights? Trying to stay awake as long as you could, trying to prevent the dance. But it wasn't ever going to end, was it?

Maybe none of it even happened. Maybe the whole thing was just a twisted dream.

Love,
Relative

April, 18th

Dear Friend,

I awoke to a second blissful morning. The sun was out as I stretched and got up from my bed. The colors of sunrise spread across a street that had only been a gloomy gray for what feels like forever.

I have coffee with the sweet woman this morning before we both go off to work at the record store. It feels nice to say that. At first, I was curious as to why she didn't invite her grandson to the coffee spot with us. I suppose she enjoys the time alone with me. I enjoy it as well.

I wrote again last night to another one of the darkest points in my life. It was hard for me to reflect on that part of my life. I wanted to scream. I wanted to throw up as the feelings came back to me. I wanted to stab something. I wanted to open my bottle, but I didn't. I figured it has to be a sober version of myself reliving those memories in order to triumph over them.

The sweet woman encouraged me not to hide from my problems by means of the gin. I felt embarrassed hearing this. Of course, she is right. I felt like my parents.

It is time for change, and I am. Rapidly and for the better.

I will write to you soon.

Your friend,
Adilyn

April, 18th

Dear Adilyn,

I am certainly proud of you for not giving into those instincts, dear girl. You are stronger than that. If you were to intoxicate while battling the memories, you wouldn't really have battled them at all. I hope you are enjoying this sunshine, but please don't forget about when there wasn't any.

Love,
Your friend

April, 18th

Dear Sweet woman,

Funny how sometimes two people can meet, and a friendship can click as if they have been friends their entire life. I cherish the fact that we have that type of situation. You told me that the lack of sunlight had always kept my brown eyes dark, but when it broke through the clouds, it made them sort of twinkle—going from the dark of an oak tree to a lighter, soft pool of honey. I smiled. I never liked my brown eyes. I was always yearning to have green eyes; I think they are the most magnificent. But you made me feel as though mine were pretty.

We talked more about your late husband. He died of what you called "old age" just a few years ago. You smiled when you talked about his passing. Obviously, not in a sinister way, but more like you were reminiscing as you spoke about him. He was a musician in more ways than one. He loved you. I could hear it in your voice. Your hand rose to your neck and clasped around the golden chain that you wear. He had given it to you.

You told me about his little sailboat, which he would take you on. It was your first date. All he needed to do was strum that guitar for you for the very first time, and you fell head over heels for him. He loved that little boat. You said you couldn't tell me how many times the first date was recreated. He loved the sunset, too. He said he would buy you a necklace and let the rays from the dying sun bounce across it. He loved you and saved money from working in a record store for a whole year to buy you the necklace you wear today. How lovely it is.

He loved his daughter, your only child. Your mood kind of dropped when you talked about her. It was a brief topic. She wanted to grow up too fast. She had a child too early. She just wasn't ready.

After we had finished our coffee, we stood up to walk over to the store—my new place of work. The place where I find myself at my genuine happiest.

Yours,
Adilyn

April, 18th

Dear Adilyn,

Bringing back some old memories of my husband was such a lovely conversation on such a lovely day, especially because of the conversation I had with my dear friend. You are so appreciated in so many ways, beautiful girl. One day, you will realize just how much.

Love,
Sweet woman

April, 18th

Dear Kind boy,

My new job doesn't really feel like work. Work feels forced, and from my experiences of the past, it can be a dreadful thing. Working with you and your grandmother is different. We have a connection similar to the one I have with her, as if we have been friends for years. All day, I was looking forward to our walk home tonight. Just like the past two times I have seen you, you offered to walk me home. I was never going to ask for it. I never will. You make me feel like I would never have to.

We talked about your childhood today as we worked. It was very much like mine in some ways and very different in others. Neither of us came from perfect homes—not that many people do—but "imperfect" is a gross understatement for the way we were brought up. You didn't go to a school like mine; you were popular. You had many friends and were involved in many things in your community.

I have never been told my laugh was pretty until today when you said so. I didn't know what to say to that. I felt my face flush. You turned away as if you didn't see to spare me the embarrassment, but I'm sure you did. We talked about the artists on the street as well. You asked if

I had ever gone and had a drawing done, and I couldn't help but lie.

We were busy again today. The sweet woman said it's typically this busy. It doesn't matter to you. You wouldn't accept any money from her even if she tried to give it to you, which I have watched her do multiple times. You are kind of like her. You are gentle as well. I noticed this when we walked back to my place once the day was done. You never even so much as grabbed my hand. This could either be because you simply didn't want to or because you didn't want to embarrass yourself by trying. If it's the latter, I must say that I find it adorable. And if it's the former, I will still happily take the walks back. I feel safe. I feel cared for.

I will see you tomorrow.
Adilyn

April, 18th

Dear Adilyn,

It does shock me how close to you I feel despite only knowing you for a couple of days. My grandmother tells me the two of you clicked this way as well. Perhaps you just have a different charisma from many people that I have met.

I do love working with you and meeting you. I do hope that we grow into being good friends soon. I hope you are comfortable with me walking you home at night as I have been the past couple of times. It puts my mind at ease to know that you are safe in that building.

I want to compliment you. I want to tell you things I feel like you deserve to hear but haven't. I just often have trouble putting those kinds of sentences together. I notice our conversations seem to hit a lull whenever I try to come up with something to say to you. Something to make you smile.

I do, however, appreciate the conversations we have had when my mind wasn't on the subject. They are good, strong conversations. And they seem to flow like butter. Reminding me of a chemistry that I had with someone that I used to know.

Even in the quiet, though, it is comfortable. I am glad to have met you, Adilyn.

Until tomorrow, angelic girl.

Love,
Kind boy

April, 18th

Dear Friend,

Do you suppose the way I am starting to feel about the sweet woman's grandson is too sudden? I don't know him all that well. Then again, I didn't know the sweet woman that well before I confided in her. Before she became my friend.

The point may be moot either way because of the very simple possibility that he doesn't feel any of the same kind of way that I do. I can accept that; I am happy for the company. The loneliness of my life is washing away like the way sand does when the waves crash up against it. It's disappearing like a train going through a tunnel.

I think waiting, letting him let me know, is the way of going about things—as if I am bold enough to initiate a conversation like that anyway.

I am going to be writing again tonight. To someone I did have feelings for long ago. It is a sad story, but it is one of my past.

Goodnight, friend
Adilyn

April, 18th

Dear Adilyn,

Had you told me just a few months ago about this situation that could potentially develop with this boy, I would have been very concerned. But recently, things are starting to change for you. You met a friend who is having amazing effects on your mental health. The sun is coming out, sweet girl. I always remind you to be careful, but that doesn't mean you shouldn't dance in the sunshine once in a while.

Love,
Your friend

April, 18th

Dear Pretty girl,

I write to you tonight because all you and I ever knew was the dark. We met at school. You were pretty, and you were popular, but you weren't like them. That school was never a place where you could stand out and be accepted. And I stood out like a sore thumb. You didn't. But I remember once we got into the higher grade levels, I would notice you to be staring at me. You didn't stare at me with disgust like the rest of them. You didn't stare and laugh at me the way the monster and his goons did in the halls after he attacked me. No, your stare was soft. It was kind.

We could only whisper, never daring to raise our voices. The boys would fall at your feet, and I would have to walk by like I didn't even notice. You were so scared of the consequences of it all. Our religious school, your conservative parents. It all terrified you. But you couldn't help it, could you? You were addicted to me the way I was to you. We could only dance in the dark because you had to hide from the light. It all became too much for you, didn't it? You let the guilt of your guiltiest pleasure twist you until you just couldn't take it anymore. I'm not mad at what you did to me, Pretty girl. I know why you did it. You had to. I don't think about you so often anymore, and I doubt you ever think of me.

I was never mad at what you did. You had an image to attend to. Part of that image was to ruin mine, like the rest of the school. Not just the students, either. Once you thought people were starting to notice, you said things, horrible things, about me as if I hadn't heard them before. As if I could let a word hurt me after everything I'd been through. You did it in front of a crowd. The crowd pressured you into doing it. I watched your heart shatter in your pretty eyes as you spit venom from your lips. I just walked away. I could feel how much it hurt you. We never spoke again after that, but I always knew.

I hope you are well
Adilyn

April, 18th

Dear Adilyn,

Oh, my love, where do I even begin? You know I loved you, or at least I hope you do. I cried every night about what had happened between us. I hated myself for it. I lost control of myself after it happened. I would watch my own blood dance along my soft silk sheets for months just to feel anything at all after it all happened. But there was nothing I could do, Adilyn! That school and the church wouldn't accept people like us. We are different from them, and that is not okay in their eyes. They needed to mold us in their perfect image, or otherwise, we were considered deviant. I could've lost everything if they had found out. You would have done the same thing as me if the roles were switched! What would the people think?

I feel you never cared what they thought. That's why they hated you so much. You were different from them. You refused the church's forced-fed ideas. And how infuriated they were because of that! But that's what drew me to you—your disregard for the rules. Your rebellious nature had me so addicted to your taste. To the way, you rubbed my virgin body. Your arms were the most heavenly place I could ever be. But, to only be loved in the shadows is a cold way to be loved.

Obviously, it was me who decided to keep us hidden. What else was I supposed to do? I wrestled with the decision for so long. I regretted what I did as soon as it happened. I wish I could take it all back. I wish I ran to you then, away from this life that was laid out for me by the writings of some book. But I cannot go back now. We cannot go back now. Sometimes, words can hurt. Other times, they can kill. I will forever be sorry, my love.

Love,
Pretty girl

April, 19th

Dear Friend,

It has been a few nights since I last awoke to my dreaded nightmare. I used to want to open my closet every day. Now, it seldom even crosses my mind. I am leaving soon to go meet the sweet woman for coffee again. She seems even happier than when I first met her. Despite her being the most joyful person I had ever met, even then. It makes me happy to see her happy. I owe her more than she will ever know. I wonder if she does. I have decided to avoid, or at least not initiate, any talks of my attraction to her grandson. I am not sure how she would take it. I don't want to ruin this special relationship I have with her over something that is very possible and never even materializes. I feel myself taking more pride in how I look. How I present myself had never really been important to me. I feel the cause of this was the importance of it being pressed onto me for much of my childhood.

Almost as if I was trying to be defiant to society, I saw no importance in it. The other cause was the lack of meaning before it. At my darkest, I found no meaning in looking nice and carrying myself with any degree of a feeling of self-worth. That is all starting to change for me now as I begin to shift my attitude as a result of these incredible events of recent. The two days I have worked at the record store would be the equivalent of three or four clients. I think I will spend the money on some nicer clothes. I must be on my way now, friend. I will write to you soon.

All of my best,
Adilyn

April, 19th

Dear Adilyn,

Behind that closet door lies defeat. You are in the same room, but so far from it now. That makes me swell with joy. That horrific dream you had been having is fading now. The sun is coming out. Finally, finally casting its rays onto you. You are beautiful in all the ways you never used to allow yourself to believe. Not that you believe them now, but I feel that you are well on your way. Keep in touch.

Love,
Your friend

April, 19th

Dear Little Street,

The road that divides the various buildings but brings the people together. Kind of like a quiet life, our little street is unknown to many. But there are tragedies here and miracles here as well. They may go unnoticed by the world.

When the lonely man sobs, his sobs are never heard. When the happy man shouts his words of joy among an already joyous crowd, his shouts go unheard as well. Not to me, though. Not to us.

Our little street is far from unimportant. People cry here, and people laugh here. Hearts are broken on the same day that smiles are formed. This street has a story just like everyone else.

To us, you are the facilitator of our stories. A place where we triumphed. A place where defeat reigned as king. Even if I dropped dead today, you have played as the setting for some of the most important parts of my story. Some small, but, oh, how they matter.

Your resident,
Adilyn

April, 19th

Dear Adilyn,

It is quite astonishing to see all the stories unfolding here. A place that not many people travel to. I am not a place where many people think they matter. The truth is, every single soul here has a story. Up and down this road, they matter. I hold the rich and the poor: the needy and the content. I have for so long. Your story seemed so grave yet so miraculous now. I noticed, even if nobody else did.

Love,
Little street

April, 19th

Dear Sweet woman,

We sat at our coffee spot, and our conversation began with more of the same. You asked me how I was doing, if I was still taming all the monstrous beasts of my past. You said you worried about how it might affect me if reliving those things became too hard on me. It is, but in a way, it is more relieving than anything. I told you it was not hard on me at all.

You, being the one who guided me in such a direction, I didn't want you to feel as if you had given me poor advice—because you truly did not. You caring for me, trying to help, and actually helping is the most I can say anyone has ever done for me.

I decided to ask you about your grandson. I asked why he was here. Your expression turned a little bit colder than it usually is. This filled me with instant regret upon bringing up the question in the first place. But you did tell me why.

What a harrowing tale it was. The boy, your grandson, had met a beautiful woman where he was living. They spent many years together, growing up with each other, and plans were set for a lovely wedding. It all fell apart, though. She left him, leaving nothing but a note.

You told me how he said he needed someplace new, where he wasn't constantly reminded of tragedy. You said you were surprised at how well he seemed to be doing, given that he truly did love that woman he used to know. You also said the unfolding of these events was the reason you were so keen on me meeting him.

I found this statement odd. What did you mean by that? I was afraid to ask, and I wondered if I had misunderstood. I left the coffee spot a little early today.

I went off to the building right next door to the record store to see about getting some new clothes. I took my time looking at the various colors of all the clothing. I felt as if wearing black is who I am, through times, good and bad. They looked nice on me, and so I decided to buy them.

I will see you at work, sweet woman.

Yours,
Adilyn

April, 19th

Dear Adilyn,

Nothing about living is easy. Even on a quiet day, we still make a flurry of decisions—sometimes without even realizing they are being made. Imperfection will last as long as there is at least one human heart still beating, for it is in each and every single one of us. It is what separates us from one another.

Once we can stare imperfection in the face, we can guide ourselves toward becoming a more perfect person.

My grandson's old lover did a horrible thing in his eyes —and in mine. But, as humans, we must recognize that it might have been her own imperfect decision-making that struck again. I cannot be mad about what she did—only saddened by the consequences of it.

Then again, I believe in every loss, there is something to be gained. What he will gain from it, I hope, will be a beautiful thing.

Only time will tell, sweet girl.

Love,
Sweet woman

April, 19th

Dear Kind boy,

I noticed you staring at me as I walked in this morning, wearing my new clothes. I put on my makeup today as well—for the first time in ages. I was nervous before I walked into the store, thinking I might have been acting strange to you, knowing what had happened.

Fortunately, we just had our conversations and did our work as we had been the past few days. I didn't expect a compliment from you, but you gave me one. Another one. For the first time in my life, I am beginning to believe people when they say kind things to me. Perhaps enough to be okay with who I am. Extrinsically for now, but progress is progress.

I watched you work today and wondered who in their right mind would do something as mad as leaving you. You are kind. You are interesting. You have a type of beauty that I have never seen before—a strong build and a soft smile. A defined face makes your green eyes stand out. I have to remind myself not to stare sometimes. Even with my own reminders, I find myself struggling.

We worked all day. The sun seemed to zoom across the sky. When it dipped beyond the horizon, and the orange and pink lights from the sunset fell away into the black of the night, the sweet woman said it was time to close down the shop. Tomorrow, we will be back. Every day has been busy, keeping the personal conversations short. I cherished them, though.

Once again, you walked me home. It wasn't as quiet as it usually is. You didn't try to hold my hand, and you never even asked for so much as a hug. When we got to the steps, we said goodbye, and once again, you strolled off into the dark.

Until tomorrow
Adilyn

April, 19th

Dear Adilyn,

In truth, the small compliments proper for a friend that I give you are starting to kill me. I want to tell you that you enthrall me with your beauty. But what a thing to say! To someone I just met. Someone I hardly know anything about.

I mean, it is insane! Have I gone insane? Wanting to be with you so soon and so badly? But I have been hurt, dear girl. I have been poisoned by the vicious venom that spits with something as soft as cold words. Now, I have walls up around my heart.

I have found that maybe nobody is deserving of the love I can give. It is never me who decides this. It is the actions they take that decide it for me. And I feel that once I do find someone deserving of the love I can give, would they really want it?

For now, I will just stand here next to you. Working in my grandmother's record store. Having the small conversations that drive me up the wall. I will wait.

Goodnight, pretty girl.

Love,
Kind boy

April, 19th

Dear Friend,

Would it really be so outrageous for me to make a move on the kind boy? I know what it feels like to get my heart broken. I know what he is going through. It is a truly horrible thing—enough to make a person never want to put themselves out there again.

Even when they do, it puts walls up. It makes a person never want to give another person the chance to break their heart again. Even if they are interested in someone, they suppress it with fear. They build a strong demeanor and wonder if anyone deserves their love.

The heartbroken have so much to give, but they wonder if anyone would even want it.

I don't want to create an awkward situation that stems from my feelings toward him. I do not even know if he would be interested in me. But I see the way his green eyes look at me when he doesn't think I can tell. They move up and down my body slowly as if inspecting it— or yearning for it.

I watch his face when he talks to me. He seems nervous, in a truly adorable fashion, of course. I am no stranger to nervousness, but I can hide it better than he can.

We moved through another day of sunshine today. I am beginning to feel more and more confident as the ink continues to glide. I am staying away from my bottle. I will continue my nightly trend of writing about my past. Another opportunity to write about the horrors of my past. Another opportunity to slay the beasts that roam within the inners of my mind.

I will write to you tomorrow.

Yours,
Adilyn

April, 19th

Dear Adilyn,

From oak-strong marriages that have sprawled sixty years to the note a schoolboy passes to his crush, there have been a billion love stories in this world. They are all so different—where they take place, how long they last, or even where they are in the world.

No two love stories are alike.

One thing that they all share, though, is that at some point, somewhere around the beginning, someone told another person how pretty they are.

Love,
Your friend

April, 19th

Dear Alcoholism,

There is a certain feeling about nighttime after heavy rainfall. It feels muggy and tough to walk in, as if you have to trudge through it. While it hasn't rained in a few days, the air of the night still feels this way because of how long and hard the rain fell when it was here. The night you threw your wrath on me, the hardest, wasn't a night like tonight. The air was stale and cold. It was Christmas Eve, sometime during my childhood. My family had been over for dinner at the house. My relatives had been there too, but it was never a problem when there were so many people around. The drinks were pouring that night for everyone, but especially for my parents. This scared me because of how out of control they seemed that night.

Of course, they kept their problem hidden from the world. Only I knew of it. Only I was to suffer. Not that night. My father's excessive drinking had enraged my mother. My mother was also very intoxicated herself. They stood out on the lawn after everyone had left. I hid in my spot. It felt so normal for me to hide in my spot. It was some sick routine that I had to accept because it was necessary for my safety. I would hide, and they would wake up the next morning, seemingly totally unremembering the events that had occurred only the night before. This is when I felt the safest.

The worst times were after the sun had fallen. I never needed to hide during the day. But I sat in my spot and listened to them yell back and forth in their drunken state. It was too cold to be outside, but I doubt either of them noticed. Tears started to form in my eyes and then streamed down my soft, young face. I had watched the other kids at school, everyone buttoned up in their uniforms, talking about Christmas. They seemed so excited. I didn't really understand why because, at the time, I thought my Christmas was no different than anyone else's. I knew it would be more of the same as any year, but for some reason, I held out a false hope. I let their lush stories get to me. Tales of fireplaces and a Christmas tree swam in my mind in the days leading up. They would tell me of the Christmas stories their parents would tell them as they got tucked in.

As they got tucked in. And here I was, sobbing. Sobbing because my parents were out in the cold, fighting about something they wouldn't even remember in the morning. My mother never yelled at my father when he would try to hunt me down from one of my hiding spaces. No, she only got upset when he damaged her image to the guests. I guess she was just a less obvious drunk than he was. I cried, and I swore to never let you get to me. But you did. For years, you became my coping mechanism. I became the very thing that I feared most about Mommy and Daddy.

I am less reliant on you nowadays. I don't need your help anymore. I have not had a reason to drink in days. I have been facing me all on my own. You had my parents. You crippled them. You shall not have me.

Adilyn

April, 19th

Dear Adilyn,

I never met to embarrass you, dear girl. This is a tough world, too tough for many. Too tough for your parents, wasn't it? They couldn't get by without me. But they couldn't get far because of me either. As for you, I never meant to have hold of you the way I did. I know you despised me. I know that I was also the only thing that would bring you peace. Did it bring you peace when your problems began to spin away? Did you find peace once your eyes began to gleam? I hope you did. I was only ever trying to help. I am glad you can walk away from me now. I am glad that you don't have to hide anymore.

Love,
Alcoholism

April, 20th

Dear Happiness,

I don't believe we have met. Not for this long of a period of time, at least. I didn't think we ever would. You are here now, though. Hopefully, you are here to stay.

Hoping that you never leave
Adilyn

April, 20th

Dear Adilyn,

I am glad you are here, my child. I wish to warm you. I will heal your aching body so long as you stay with me. I am here now. You are safe.

Love,
Happiness

April, 20th

Dear Friend,

I plan on being in the good graces of the sweet woman this morning as we have our daily meeting. The sun is out, and it is smiling at the world beneath it. I wrote to another one of the darker sides of my past last night. It feels good that these things have less and less of an impact on me as I write to them. With every line from every letter, the bad starts to fade away. Just as my nightmare is, the details that were frozen inside of my brain have just vanished. Leaving nothing but a foggy cloud. My clothes were folded and ready for me on my dresser this morning. Usually, I just leave them on the floor and re-wear them until I cannot stand them anymore. Every day is getting better—something I am not used to but am brilliantly happy to report it.

I will write soon,
Adilyn

April, 20th

Dear Adilyn,

Such lovely news! You are so beautiful. Every day that you take care of yourself and take pride in yourself will bring you closer to seeing just how beautiful you are.

Love,
Your friend

April, 20th

Dear Artist,

There we all were again. The sweet woman and I enjoying our coffee, and you setting up for another day of work. Part of me imagines that business would fall a little bit for you now that the sun is out. I would just think that people would be a little more desperate for something beautiful to look at when the world around them is so bleak.

Maybe it will just draw more people to you instead. Perhaps some people would want something beautiful to keep them warm in case the clouds ever roll back in. Something to hold on to just to remember a sunny day.

I can see clearly, though, that you wouldn't care if you sold a hundred paintings in one day or if you just sold one. I can see your goal is just to give people a little sunshine, whether it is outside or not.

All of my best,
Adilyn

April, 20th

Dear Adilyn,

Precious girl, I will have you someday soon. You will sit in this chair and let me show you all of your beauty. It is all there, you just need someone to guide you to see it.

Love,
Artist

April, 20th

Dear Friend,

Oh, my lovely friend, what a day it was. My head is spinning with emotion, and I do not even really know where to start with the explanation of it all. I suppose I will start at the beginning. It started off relatively the same as it typically does. I had no reason to think anything different of it. I took a little longer than usual to get ready, caring a bit more than I had in the past. I took a little more pride in myself. I strode out of my room and down the stairs into the lobby, passing by the grand mirror. I still cannot manage to give it a look. Once I pushed open the heavy doors to the building, I had to squint because of the sunlight that covered my eyes. This was such a forgotten and welcomed feeling ever since the sunshine went away.

I passed by the man on the street and gave him a smile. He met mine with the same foggy smile that I receive every time. I sat and had coffee with the sweet woman. We listened to some other people behind us witter on about this and that. We shared a few laughs of our own, discussing the store and the customers who come in. We watched the artist set up her station, and then we walked right past her into the store. Here, we met up with the kind boy. He was offering assistance to some younger customers trying to purchase a few records from the shelves. I watched him as he worked. We sat together as he tinkered with one of the broken record players someone had brought in. He even showed me some of how the machine worked and explained how to fix it once he had located the issue.

After that, the store got very busy. The sweet old lady was held by a countless number of customers at her desk, buying and selling records and a few record players. I figured I ought to offer some assistance tending to the drive of people since sweeping and straightening the store was of less importance than the people's current needs. After what felt like an eternity, it was time to close up for the day. The last few people shuffled out, and the sweet woman had gone upstairs to nurse her exhaustion from the shift. The kind boy and I talked a little but mostly wrapped up the things we needed to complete before I returned to my building. I swept, straightened, and dusted the shelves. He put the records back on display for the window and the record player that he fixed behind the desk where the sweet woman sits.

The sun had long dipped beyond the horizon by the time it was time to leave. And without fail, the kind boy asked to walk me home yet again. We walked in silence, the type of silence that is screaming to be broken, but nobody can think of what to say. He seemed nervous to walk with me tonight, more nervous than typical for him. We stopped in front of my building, near the man on the street who was audibly sleeping up against the wall. I wanted him to say something to me—anything at all. I was internally begging for him to speak. But I bore just a smile on the outside. I didn't want to let my disappointment turn into rudeness, so I offered him a polite goodbye and turned to grab the door handle of my building.

When I turned to do this, I almost jumped when I felt his hand grab mine. He pulled me away from the door and into his chest, and that's when our lips locked in just the way I had fantasized throughout these past few days. What a moment it was. Even the noise of the man on the street, not ten feet away, could be heard. All the moments I had cried, the fear of being woken up by that horrible dream, the cruelty of every recipient of the letters I sent, it was all gone. His hands started around my waist as he pulled me in. From there, they glided down further and then up again to the back of my head. My question was, was he a good kisser too? He paused for a moment after the first time our lips touched, as if to make sure I was okay with what he had done. I knew that I had been his since the moment I saw him, but his wanting to make sure that I was alright only made me all the more attracted to him.

He was soft and gentle, brushing my hair behind my neck as we stood there wrapped in each other, but still passionate, still strong. I didn't want him to go. I didn't want that moment to end. I wasn't worried about anything in that second; the euphoria had pulled me into something of a wild race, even though I was already a step from the finish line. I pulled away from his lovely face and pulled hard on his arms. I guided him into the lobby, past the mirror. I took him up the stairs and into my room, letting his strong body fling me onto my bed. He shut the door behind him and followed me to the spot where I lay awaiting all that he could give me.

Once he met me where I was sitting, he took his time with my body. Not a word was spoken the entire time; there were no words to be spoken. Like the thunderous crashing of a thousand waves onto a thousand beaches, our passion for each other roared on into a warm night. It was sensational. He took me to places I had never been before. How beautiful of a thing it was—something I had dreamed of, managing to fulfill every promise I had thought of. Once the final ember skipped from the fire that had just blazed, he stood up, and we recollected ourselves. We sat there on the edge of the bed, and for the first time all day, it seemed we had hit our conversational spark. We talked, we giggled, and the nervousness that saturated the air since we had first met each other seemed to have all but dissipated. He held me close as we sat on the edge of my bed, looking at the record player that couldn't seem to drown me out tonight.

Eventually, the time had beckoned him to leave. He told me he would've stayed all night if he hadn't worried that his grandmother would fret. I told him never to mind that, walked him back into the warm night air, and wished him a safe walk back. My legs shook hard as I walked back to my room. My body, mind, and soul seemed to be tangled with shock. I sat in a content silence alone in my room for a while after he left. Dreaming replaying the whole night over and over in my head. I revisited every single move he made. Feeling his touch even an hour after he was gone. I sit here now, writing to you. Feeling free, feeling happy.

Hoping you are well
Adilyn

April, 20th

Dear Adilyn,

Sweet girl, how happy I am for you. I know of all your terrible stories when it comes to intimacy. It is so beautiful that you finally have a treasured one. You are so special. I hope he continues to make you feel that way.

Love,
Your friend

April, 20th

Dear Sex,

It has been because of you that I have often felt disgusting. You have left me humiliated and ashamed. Uncomfortable in my own skin after the things that have happened to me. Unwanted and unattractive, used and hidden by those who didn't want others to know what they had done to or with me. A catalyst for my nightmare, I never thought of you as something beautiful. Now, I stand corrected. With the right person, what a lovely thing you are. What an experience it was to be so entangled in him. Knowing, for once, that it was pure. It was free, with no darker agenda beneath. No reason to hide me. I welcome this new perspective on you. I am appreciative of it.

Adilyn

April, 20th

Dear Adilyn,

I can be a beautiful thing if that is what I am meant to be. I am sorry for the way you have been treated through me. Nobody should have to experience me in such a terrible way. You deserve to be given intimacy in ways as beautiful as you. Nothing less.

Love,
Sex

April, 20th

Dear Kind boy,

Here I lay wishing only for you to have stayed. It does, however, ease my consciousness that you went home so that your grandmother wouldn't worry. That sweet woman has done miracles for me with only a few simple conversations as her method. I wouldn't wish her to worry about anything for the rest of her days. I can feel my heart racing as I write to you. My body is still twitching from our dance. It is funny how I didn't want to put any pressure on our relationship to be anything more than platonic. I suppose plans can change. I will meet with the sweet woman tomorrow morning for our coffee. Wishing you the sweetest of dreams, my kind boy.

Yours,
Adilyn

April, 20th

Dear Adilyn,

Beautiful girl, you are so amazing to me. The way you walk, the way you talk. The way your hair falls down your back. Your touch is addicting, and I will stay addicted forever.

Love,
Kind boy

April, 21st

Dear Friend,

I rose to another bright day this morning. I felt a different feeling this morning than the one I have grown accustomed to. The feeling of disgust and self-loathing that I typically feel after a guest occupies my room the previous night has evaporated. What a freeing feeling it is! I am unsure of the repercussions of what I have done. I do not think that I will tell the sweet woman. I find it odd how content I feel this morning. I do not fear that the kind boy was only after what I had given to him last night. I could see it in his eyes, a want for something deeper. I would like that as well. There are many things that I am numb to, but the use others have with my body is not one of them. I believe there will be gestures to follow. I believe I will not hold an ounce of regret for what I have done.

Best wishes,
Adilyn

April, 21st

Dear Adilyn,

Another day of sunshine is a good thing. I hope you do not regret last night. I think only good things will come from it.

Love,
Your friend

April, 21st

Dear Sweet woman,

We will meet for coffee in an hour. I wonder if you were awake when the kind boy returned to your apartment atop the record store. I doubt you would even tell me had you noticed the hour of his arrival. I hardly think it will be an issue, though. I realize you probably only wish for joy for the people you care for. And the joy meeting the both of you has brought me is immense.

Once again, I take my time before rushing off to leave. My clothes are straightened with care. My hair is brushed as well. I want to believe the words that you and your grandson tell me each day. It seems a little less impossible these days. Maybe someday soon.

See you soon,
Adilyn

April, 21st

Dear Adilyn,

I had a feeling when I went to rest last night that I would be home alone for some time. I see that I was correct. I wish for you to believe the kind of things you are told. You deserve to.

Love,
Sweet woman

April, 21st

Dear Kind boy,

Despite the unusual calm that I have felt ever since the events of last night, I couldn't seem to shake a trickle of nervousness that there would be some kind of awkward tension between us today at the record store. Once I saw your face, however, I knew there was no reason to think that way. The endeavors I have been through with faces of old have left me ill-equipped to fully accept any romance as pure.

I once knew a pretty girl who didn't dare look me in the eyes once the sun shone onto us. I once knew a monster who took everything from me and could only offer me a chilling passing sneer. I have known not the names, but the faces rather, of clients who have passed through without ever admitting so much as a nod. But today, I walked into the record store, and we locked eyes.

I may have smiled first, but I believe that you smiled harder. Maybe I shouldn't have looked your way when you were assisting a customer. I suppose they probably wondered why your face flushed red. But maybe I couldn't help but stare at you while you worked. That is something I am sure you have realized by now.

We were busy yet again today. I was glad to see the sweet woman so active. I was worried after she had looked so worn following yesterday's shift. She seemed okay today, though.

Your grandmother has been very pleased with the sales we have made over the past few days. She told me she was so thankful for the extra help. She said she couldn't have fathomed the store doing this well until you and I began working there. She then told me that because of the good state of the store, she has decided to stay closed tomorrow. As a reward for the work we have done. She said a bit of time off would be a good thing for us.

The sun sped across the sky today. Casting its bright rays all around this place that was dark for so long. Once it vanished, you asked to walk me home again. While bold, I decided to ask about the girl that had left you. You told me about her vaguely, as if you were talking about a stranger. Or a memory you were trying hard to forget. I would think that you are. You didn't seem upset that I had asked about her, but I figured I better not do it again.

I silently hoped to myself last night that you are not only after what you have already had from me, and I do think that is the case. You walked me to the doors of my building, and we shared another kiss—this one marking a goodbye for the day at least. You gave me one last shy smile and then turned around and walked off into the night.

Goodnight, Kind boy,
Adilyn

April, 21st

Dear Adilyn,

Working with you is an incredible joy, pretty girl. I am glad there was never a moment of awkwardness between us. We have seemed to move past that. I am still nervous around you, and I wonder if there will ever be a day when I am not.

Love,
Kind boy

April, 21st

Dear Friend,

There lies fear in my heart that all this is too good to be true. It presses down on me, making me worry that I could lose it all in an instant. After spending nearly all my life drowning, why is it now that I am finally able to breathe? How have I been so fortunate to have been sent these loving people?

I do know, however, that being crippled by fear could bring that instant closer—an instant that may never come. I have the power to create it. Rather, the darker forces that try to control me have the power to shove me stumbling into it. I must fight them; I must find control.

It is true that I did not write last night, as the sweet woman instructed me to do so—not to confront something that lurks in my past. I was distracted, as you can imagine. But tonight, that will change. I have more to say, and I will say it. I will launch my cutting words right into the bellies of my beasts. I want to watch them bleed out once and for all. And I will.

Yours,
Adilyn

April, 21st

Dear Adilyn,

Never sway yourself off a good path because fear drives you in the wrong direction. Hold onto the good, and more shall come. I am proud of you for writing again tonight. Once the door is shut on these evils, they cannot come back to haunt you any longer.

Love,
Your friend

April, 21st

Dear Monster,

How dare you do what you did to me? What kind of scum has the absence of consciousness to be able to handle the weight of doing what you did? Pure evil.

But you didn't hurt me, did you, Monster? No, you hurt her. You hurt a shy girl, a lonely and quiet girl. One that was uncomfortable in her own skin. Too embarrassed to try and make a friend. Too unloving of herself to have any confidence. You left her screaming, sobbing in her bathroom, trying to wash the feeling of you off her body.

You hurt a sweet girl; you ruined her, didn't you? You tried. You wanted to. She was the one with the panic attacks, she was the one who had to suffer while her head spun out. She was the one who had to tell herself to put the knife down while alone in her bedroom because nobody else cared enough to tell her to.

You hurt her. Not me.

So go ahead, monster. Walk around with your fangs tucked behind your lips. Your claws shoved deep into your pockets. You tried to murder a loving girl. But you couldn't because there has never been a moment where you have been stronger than she.

You may have taken the light from her eyes, but a fire sparked that night when you did. A fire in her eyes that will burn your twisted body. Burn it and burn it until all you are is ash.

Die,
Adilyn

April, 22nd

Dear Friend,

When I stir awake these mornings of recent, I cannot help but smile. The letter I wrote last night killed a part of me that will never truly die. The letter I wrote was one intended for one of the most heinous "people" I have ever known. That night will stay with me forever, but the Monster is dead. He won't reign power over me any longer. I will not allow it.

I smile because I am beginning to cut the weight that has pulled on me. I smile because I am able to breathe again.

I do not have much, my friend. But I do have a friend. I do have a kind boy. I do have the aspects of life that I have always seemed to miss out on. I feel that those aspects are all that I have ever really needed in order to begin making my peace.

I am finding my own way into happiness.

Best wishes,
Adilyn

April, 22nd

Dear Adilyn,

Look how far you have come! The door is shut on that dreadful night. The sun is out now, dear girl.

Love,
Your friend

April, 22nd

Dear Man of the street,

I left my place a little earlier than I was planning because I thought it might be nice to stop by the store

and bring you something to eat. I worry your eyes grow
a little more distant each time I see you. I think I now
understand how you can smile after having so little. It
shocked me when you smiled at me on a gloomy day
when I thought such a thing to be impossible. I hope you
are enjoying this sunshine. I hope I bring you some as
well.

All of my best,
Adilyn

April, 22nd

Dear Adilyn,

When you sit where I sit, dear child, all you need is a
little sunlight. A little warmth occasionally to kill off the
cold.

Love,
Man of the street

April, 22nd

Dear Sweet woman,

A pleasant surprise was seeing your grandson sitting
with you as I made my way over for our morning
meeting. Of course, this did lead to a subsiding in you
asking about my writings. I didn't mind, though. I know
you would've asked had he not been there.

I have appreciated you not telling him the things that I have told you. I am truly an independent person, despite my promptness to open up to you. I fear what I may have done if I hadn't had a shoulder to lean on then. But I found one, and it kept me from living my nightmare.

Despite the protests from your grandson and me, you declared that today would be a good day to tidy up the record store. We said you should take the day to enjoy yourself, but you declined in anticipation of busy days ahead. I did, however, convince both of you to let me pay for the coffee, which left me satisfied.

After you left, your grandson asked if I would like to spend the day with him. Of course, I obliged, and we sat and planned our day together.

I will see you tomorrow, sweet woman.

Yours truly,
Adilyn

April, 22nd

Dear Adilyn,

I do wonder how your writing is going. Hopefully, well, it is of the utmost importance that you continue to bring down those evil forces in your life. I hope you and my grandson have a wonderful day today. I will see you soon, sweet girl.

Love,
Sweet woman

April, 22nd

Dear Kind boy,

What a lovely day I had with you. Our day in the sun was no less than anything that I had hoped for it to be. We stayed at the coffee shop for a while and talked about all sorts of things. I know that a conversation isn't the most exciting way to spend time, but there are few events in this world that I would trade for a good conversation. It is nice to have someone as comfortable as you are to talk to.

I told you about stories from my past. You told me some from yours. Neither one of us dared to step foot into a story deeper than surface level, probably trying not to scare the other one off. You asked what I did before I came to work at the record store, and I couldn't help but lie to you. I was embarrassed. I told you I worked right here at the coffee shop. I did feel some guilt for it, but everyone has a story. Sometimes, the story you tell, even if it is your own, is different from the truth. I might tell you eventually, but not today.

We walked around our little street for a while, watching different people carry out their daily tasks. We went to the little boutique just a block from the grocery store, where I bought food for the Man of the street. I had always thought it was cute, but I had never been inside. I never had a reason to.

I didn't expect you to buy me flowers, but you did. Daisies and a beautiful vase to go with them. I cannot remember the last time I smiled so much in one day. My jaw ached from it all——in the best way I can possibly imagine. I love the words you say to me. The little things do not go unnoticed. How could they? I have never had anything more than that.

Night seemed to come crashing down on our fun in the blink of an eye. We walked back to the store and up the stairs into your quarters of the sweet woman's apartment. There, you strummed your guitar a little and sang to me as my head rested against your leg. How serene it was.

Once the time had reached a very late hour, my gentleman walked me back to my building, kissed me goodnight, and again spun off into the dark.

Thank you for today,
Adilyn

April, 22nd

Dear Friend,

In my mind, he is perfect. There is no flaw to be found. Being with him today lifted me further into my perfect world. Even if it was just for a day, it was one of the best of my life. My budding relationship with the kind boy is still incredible to me. The way he talks to me, the whispers of how lovely I look when he holds me close— it makes me feel lovely.

Tomorrow, I will meet with the sweet woman in the morning. Tonight, I will write again. Goodnight, dear friend.

Yours,
Adilyn

April, 22nd

Dear School,

To be accepting and welcoming of all people except those who do not walk and talk like you is not to be welcoming and accepting of all people. You made me out to be evil when I was just a child. A child with different ideas than the ones of which you taught to us.

Forced to pray to a god that never seemed to keep his ever-watching eyes open to watch over me. Forced to thank this god the morning after I had to hide from my father in his drunken rage the night before. Forced to appreciate him a day removed from having my innocence ripped away from me.

Where was your god when I was falling victim to a relative that my family gloried? Where was your god when my peers would torment me every day until the idea of going to school made me violently ill?

You told me that we are all god's creatures, created in his perfect image. But then you also told me that the way I thought was wrong. How I dressed was wrong.

I had to hide my love for a pretty girl at school because, in the eyes of you, that was wrong too. So, how can I have been created in his perfect image if the image I give off is all wrong? I never understood that.

But you didn't mind. As long as your students, as long as your pawns, were brainwashed with what you told them, you would be content. It never mattered how or why. Not to you, anyway.

I am free now from your chains. You will not command

the life I live. I am all on my own, with no one to worship. Nothing to pray to. And that is okay with me.

Burn,
Adilyn

April, 23rd

Dear Friend,

I am starting to lose touch with what it felt like to wake up to that horrible nightmare. I cannot really give myself a reason to want to open my closet door. I woke up as bright as the rising sun. I woke up ready to see my friend. Ready to see my kind boy. I woke up not wishing I hadn't.

Hoping you are well
Adilyn

April, 23rd

Dear Sweet woman,

Today, when you asked me if I had written any more about my past, I told you all about my letter from last night. I told you of the horrors that I faced in that school. I told you of the things that had happened to me.

You held my hand as I talked. I couldn't stop a few tears from splashing into my coffee. You gripped it tighter when I told you of the pretty girl that I used to know.

And then you grabbed my other hand as I started to lower my head and tell you about the monster.

And then I remembered the most recent letter I wrote to it, and I raised my head back up again as I spoke. We were quiet for a long while after that.

But my sweet woman, how thankful I am for you. I have never had tears wiped off my face before. I am glad I have met someone who will not let them fall.

Your friend,
Adilyn

April, 23rd

Dear Enthrallment,

Who am I to say that I am in love as I sit, unsure that I even know what that word means? Have I ever seen love? I couldn't imagine a story from my childhood where my parents acted as though they had been in it. I question if I loved the pretty girl that I once knew. I wonder if that was love or if it was just the excitement that came with the rebellious nature of our situation.

I do, however, believe that love comes in many forms. I think one person can feel love for different ideas and things in different ways. I love the sweet woman—not romantically, of course—but I love her for the way she has become a pillar of strength for me in a life where I have lacked such pillars. I love my record player, even if it is simply an inanimate object. There is life to it, a spirit that it carries as it wards off the feelings of loneliness and the troubling silence that fills my room when the sun has set.

I do not know if I love the kind boy. Maybe it takes time, more time than I have even known him. But I am enthralled with him, his appearance, his mind. The way he says all the words to me is something that I have trouble accepting as true. My enthrallment of him is large. It devours me.

Perhaps it is love, and I am just unaware of it. Or untrusting of it. For now, my enthrallment with him will suffice. It will expand as it does every day. And one day, I will fall deeply in love. I will fall when I become ready to let myself do so.

Adilyn

April, 23rd

Dear Kind boy,

Your words and actions continue to astonish me every day. The three of us worked a long day in the record store. There has been a considerable decrease in the number of people who have been coming in, but there was still enough to make for a very busy day. As we were closing up the shop, you said you had something that you wanted to show me. All I was expecting was for us to walk back to my building, but I followed you up the stairs instead.

We went past the sweet woman's room, where she was getting ready for bed, and into the room you have been living in. From there, you began to look up at your ceiling and ran your hand along it until it rested on some type of handle with a latch. You pushed it open, and a small portion of your ceiling opened up to a beautiful night sky. There wasn't a cloud anywhere to be seen. You helped me up, putting your hands on either side of my waist until I was far enough to where I could pull myself the rest of the way.

Once I was up in the night sky, I offered you my hand so you could get up, but you declined. Using the edges of the square hole that had become a portal to the outside, you lifted yourself up with majesty and sat down beside me on the roof. The stars gleamed with such an excellence that I have never been so fortunate to witness. All the things I could see from up there! I could see the cherry blossom and the coffee shop. If I squinted and stared hard, I could make out the peaceful figure of the man of the street lying asleep in his spot.

We spent hours up there, on top of the world. Immersing ourselves in one another in our conversations. Stealing kisses as soft as the rain when our words seemed to hit a lull. You said something to me after the hours had skipped by that I will never forget. It left me shocked and speechless, unable to muster a reply for too many moments.

In the quiet dead of night, as we sat up above all the lights of the world, three words I had never heard uttered to me. Three brave words, nervous words. Three words I would never have had the courage to say to you. But I said them back once I finally found myself verbal again. I said them, and my stomach seemed to rise out of my chest. My heartbeat increased to the fastest speed I had felt in a long time.

After that, we just sat there for another half an hour or so. It wasn't an awkward silence, but it was a heavy one. One that I was comfortable with. If it were me who had spoken those words to you, I would have suffered in worry that I had gone too far. I would have relapsed with anxiety that I have been working hard to suppress, that it all was too sudden and couldn't possibly be true.

Kind boy, you need not let those troubles invade your mind. You have me, now and forever.

Goodnight, my love,
Adilyn

April, 23rd

Dear Friend,

I was unaware of how much time had passed as I sat on the roof with that kind boy. Every single step I took on our walk home seemed to be aided by a cloud. It may have been the way the stars were shining on us or the words he said to me as our night drew to a close, but I believe them now. I can say that wholeheartedly.

When the kind boy calls me beautiful, I believe that I am. When the sweet woman delivers her words of wisdom and kindness to me, I believe those words, too. I didn't change much. I just found who I needed to open me to the truth. To give me the confidence that I had lacked for so long.

Tonight, I plan to close another dark chapter capable of bringing me down. I will get stronger each time I do so.

Wishing you well,
Adilyn

April, 23rd

Dear Attempt,

I would like to imagine, as any child would, that my parents did care whether I lived or died. I would not like to imagine the sight of my mother standing in front of her bathroom mirror after learning of my passing. I did not want to imagine her standing there, shaking and crying. Creating some monstrosity of herself in her mind. Only believing that it was her fault alone.

Of course, it wasn't her fault alone. It was a myriad of events and truths that I had lived that had led me to the conclusion that I should attempt such a thing. For a while, I hated the fact that I wasn't able to go through with it. Keeping myself alive afterward for reasons unbeknownst to me.

I feel there, but there would have been people I would have never gotten to meet. There are stars that I would have never gotten to see. I have journeyed into a headspace where I am nothing but glad that you failed. I have no hate for what I did. It helped me mold into who I am now.

I wish I could tell the girl who tried where I am now. The people I know now. But she wasn't this strong yet. She wouldn't have even believed me. I am just starting to believe it myself.

Adilyn

April, 24th

Dear Friend,

I was just getting used to the light from the sunrise filling my room in the morning. Today, it was limited by some clouds that had formed in the sky. I am off now, off to go and meet the sweet woman for coffee. I will write soon.

Best regards,
Adilyn

April, 24th

Dear Sweet woman,

I arrived at the coffee shop around our usual time and was surprised not to see you there. It hasn't been often that I am the first of us to sit down. I watched the people on our little street for a while. I watched the clouds come and begin to hang over my head. I watched for you but to no avail. Finally, I did see a familiar face —that of the kind boy. I stood up as he walked briskly towards me. He looked a little down, something I was not accustomed to seeing from him. No bright smile met my eyes as he gestured for me to have a seat once again.

He told me of your exhaustion, and he said you had been tired from the string of busy days we have endured at the record store. Your grandson and I will tend to the store while you rest.

Hoping to see you soon,
Adilyn

April, 24th

Dear Kind boy,

I was initially worried that without the sweet woman to help us, our efforts would be stretched too thin today at the store. These worries subsided and were replaced with utter boredom as there were never two separate customers in the store at the same time. Time slugged by as opposed to its usual lightning speed. After a few more maddeningly dull hours, we decided to close up shop for the day.

Following this, we set off for a walk down the street. You had asked me about the street artist when you saw her working. You asked me if I had ever had a portrait done of myself. I laughed when I said no, and you turned to me with a quizzical look on your face and asked me why not.

Moments later, I was in a chair I had never thought I would be able to sit in, watching the giver of many smiles paint mine onto a canvas. Her work was beautiful. I sat there in that chair and tried to suppress a tear with all my might. I think she could tell. I'm sure the tears wouldn't have hindered her work. She works to capture smiles, not to illuminate frowns.

It felt like forever sitting across from her. It felt surreal. She was putting a face I once could never stand onto her canvas. How light I felt. When she was done, she flipped the canvas around, and I saw my face from her perspective. No suppression could hold the flow of droplets down my face when she turned that canvas around. Look how beautiful she made me out to be.

You looked worried and confused when I cried in front of her. She looked at me only with a gentle smile. Thank you, kind boy, for leading me here to this chair, where I finally was able to witness such a beautiful thing.

April, 24th

Dear Artist,

When all there was on this little street was gloom, you were still lighting up the faces of everyone who sat in your chair. I couldn't bring myself to do it. I never wanted to have to face me until I was pushed into doing so.

You have seen me at my darkest and my brightest, and today, you painted my smile when I have been doing nothing but letting it shine. You showed me how I am in the eye of a stranger, and I have nothing to be ashamed of.

I am beautiful.

Thank you,
Adilyn

April, 24th

Dear Mirror,

The kind boy and I shared a kiss goodnight outside of the doors to my building, and then he strode off back to the record store. I watched him until the outline of his body had vanished, and then I stared long and hard at the last place it was visible. I knew what I had to do once I walked inside of my building. I knew you were perched on the wall in all of your glory. Begging for me now instead of your usual sneers.

I will not bow my head as I walk by tonight. I opened the heavy doors to my building and walked inside. At first, I stood in front of you with my eyes fixed upon my shoelaces. And then I looked up. I locked eyes with the eyes I had hidden from for so long.

A mirror whose view I had dodged since I first came into this building. A lovely girl stared back at me. One who wouldn't be beaten by the horrors she had faced. One proud now of how she looked.

I stared at a girl who wanted to be as invisible to the world as she felt. She is visible now, and that is all she wants to be.

You have triumphed,
Adilyn

April, 24th

Dear Friend,

A whirlwind of a day this was. I was excited to see my friend this morning and then disappointed and worried when I learned of her condition.

I was happy to have spent time in the store with the kind boy, despite the fact that there was so little work that needed to be done. I never thought I would be in the chair across from the artist, and I certainly never thought I could face that mirror down in the lobby.

I am stronger now than I used to be. I will only continue to be.

Yours truly,
Adilyn

April, 24th

Dear Anxiety,

What could you possibly throw at me now? I am surrounded by people who love and care for me. I can face myself. I can look in the mirror, and when I do, I feel as beautiful as the kind and gentle people who have been telling me that I am.

I can sit in my silence and use it as something wondrous —a tool to reminisce about the life I have been living recently. I have no loneliness to wallow in, nothing to worry about.

You have been perpetual, but now you are being beaten.

Adilyn

April, 25th

Dear Friend,

More clouds than yesterday are covering the sky. I am hoping they will drift away and not give us any more rain. How disappointing that would be. I am not sure how the sweet woman is feeling. I think I ought to take a walk down to the record store and check on her. I will write soon.

Sincerely,
Adilyn

April, 25th

Dear Sweet woman,

A sickening feeling of unease crept upon me as I knelt by your bedside today alongside your grandson. You looked pale and gaunt. You insisted that you were just fine, but you coughed as you said it, twisting my stomach into a thousand knots.

I asked the kind boy if he would like me to stay and help him tend to you, as clearly the store would stay closed today. He thanked me but said no and went on to tell me he would rather care for you alone.

I will not allow myself to imagine the worst, as I tend to do. I have always trusted the words you have told me, and if you say you are okay, then I will believe that you are.

But I do hope that you are. I hope that with everything I have in me.

April, 25th

Dear Friend,

I had not really kept track of how much money I had been spending ever since I asked the sweet woman for a job at her record store. With it being slow and closed recently, I have not been taking very much money at all. My purchases of new clothes, food for the man of the street, and the painting done by the artist have left me quite strapped for money.

Hopefully, the sweet woman will be back on her feet soon so that we can re-open for business. I am not sure what to do with myself today. I am off of my routine of having coffee and then going down to the store.

I suppose I will write to pass the time.

Best wishes,
Adilyn

April, 25th

Dear Friend,

Hours have passed since I returned from the record store, and my mind is racing too fast to be able to concentrate on my letters. I cannot lose the sweet woman; I cannot be left shattered again. The clouds continue to pile into the sky. My record player spins in the corner as I stop these tears from sliding down my cheeks.

Yours,
Adilyn

April, 25th

Dear Silence,

The instant my walls soften, you are back to invade them. You have been so good to me recently, and I enjoyed your presence.

Now, here I am again. Unwillingly using you as a vessel for the most horrible made-up scenarios of what may happen to the sweet woman. And even if they don't happen, the record store being closed has left me in need of money. It makes me want to vomit, even beginning to think that I may possibly have to return to that evil job. I simply cannot.

My record player spins. It will drown you out.

Let me be
Adilyn

April, 26th

Dear Friend,

I didn't sleep much last night. I was awaiting a knock from the sweet boy and waiting for him to burst into my room and tell me that his grandmother was going to be okay. Waiting for him to walk into my room and tell me at least we can open the store again. That I won't have to return to that dreaded job; there was no knock on my door. There weren't even so much as footsteps in the hall. The world remained silent. I don't plan to leave my room today. I don't know where I would go. The clouds are growing darker outside, echoing a sinister promise of rain. Rain that I must stay out of.

Regards,
Adilyn

April, 26th

Dear Sweet woman,

I want to run to you and grab your hand the way you held mine when I cried to you. My beautiful woman, please do not let me be. Please do not leave me here alone.

Please
Adilyn

April, 26th

Dear Man of the street,

I have not eaten anything in two days. What guilts me the most is that I know this means that you haven't either. The kind boy has still yet to bring me any news. Every second that passes without him makes my thoughts fall deeper into a blanket of despair. Every second that passes makes the clouds a little darker. It makes me a little more desperate. I felt physically sick thinking about what had to be done, but I figured it was all in my head. That is when I vomited at the thought of it. But my desperation outweighs this sick feeling that I have. I know what I have to do.

April, 26th

Dear Record player,

I have not needed you to spin for me in many nights the way I will need you for this one. It feels surreal having this as my only option when everything was going so well. I am sick. I am disgusted. But I need you tonight.

Thank you,
Adilyn

April, 27th

Dear Friend,

We are back to the place I was so angsty to be free from. How dark my room was this morning as the rain drizzled outside. How dark my thoughts were as I woke up to that hideous dream once again.

I made enough money to buy food for myself and the man of the street. I think that is enough for me to keep my head up. I have gotten through this before; I can do it again. I do see light at the end of this tunnel.

I keep wishing for a knock on my door from that kind boy. A knock where I can let him in, and he can hold me and tell me everything will be okay. I will wish for it with everything that I have.

My best,
Adilyn

April, 3rd

Dear Friend,

How ridiculous I sound, writing about a knock that obviously will never come. But wouldn't it have been so lovely? Wouldn't it all have been lovely? Look at the mess I have made of this room. Two hundred or so letters strewn across the floor. I have spent the whole day writing them. Letters from the twisted words of loneliness. And letters from the wicked call of death. Letters of love, of fear. Letters to me from a world that I so lovingly imagined.

Eventually, the time wore on, and I rushed to get to the end of my story. I couldn't remember how the responses from the world were supposed to go. I never had many from the life that I lived. Some are horribly written and lay crumpled in their spot of rest after I threw them across the room. Some are beautiful letters, and they sit next to my ajar closet door.

I step over my broken glass figurine and look at the spot I would have loved for a record player to go. I peer out of my window and see the sawed-off stump that I transformed into a swaying cherry blossom. I will never have known a sweet woman to whom I will become a friend. I will have never known a kind boy to whom I will fall in love. I have completely fallen out of touch with this world, and it is far too late to save me.

I would have even continued with my story had the time not moved so quickly. How romantic would it have been for some daisies from the boy I loved to fight off the loneliness? How beautiful it would have been to have an artist to show me the most perfect version of myself.

How nice it would have been to be able to write to a distant friend who cared about me with such importance.

I envisioned some truly beautiful people. I passionately wrote about my dream and this closet, knowing that my dream would be realized and my closet would be opened before a new day was born. All those sad stories that I wrote were all true. But the happy ones were only part of this dreamlike story that I have written. These letters surround me now.

I fear there are a million who feel the way I do—looking for escape by any means possible. Looking for refuge, however, they can. From the silence and loneliness, from all the horrors that haunt them. My nightmare was no nightmare. It was no dream. It is only the way for me to escape. There are a million monsters out there who have destroyed a million stares into a mirror—a million pretty girls who have to hide in shadows so that they are not seen. There are a million people who could help and don't even know it.

I wanted to think of names for them, but I figured if they were nameless, they could be anybody. I must go now, my friend. The contents of my closet pull me just as I was pulled that night down by the pond. I am running out of time. I must rest my head for a minute before I escape.

It is so dark, this world when my eyes are shut. But it somehow gets darker when they open again. A quarter of an hour from now, the serenity of my room will be indescribable. I mean this literally, for I won't be able to describe it. All due to the simple fact that a quarter of an hour from now, I will have finally found my silence.

How sad is it, my friend, that there were never going to
be any sunnier days?

Goodbye, friend,
Adilyn